The CASE of the GOLDEN HELMET

TED BALLANTYNE

FriesenPress

Suite 300 - 990 Fort St
Victoria, BC, V8V 3K2
Canada

www.friesenpress.com

First Edition — 2020

Edited by Mary Metcalfe

The Case of the Golden Helmet is a work of fiction. All names, characters, places, and incidents are purely products of the writer's imagination. Any actual places or names of real people are purely coincidental and are used fictitiously.

ISBN
978-1-5255-8202-8 (Hardcover)
978-1-5255-8203-5 (Paperback)
978-1-5255-8204-2 (eBook)

1. *Fiction, Mystery & Detective, International Mystery & Crime*

Distributed to the trade by The Ingram Book Company

Contents

Author's Note

My debut novel follows a Canada Revenue Agency Special Investigator tracking down a tax cheat who not only doesn't pay his taxes, but uses a false identity to move money offshore. The **Prologue** is based on my own experience as a junior auditor with Revenue Canada some forty years ago. I referred the file to Special Investigations for their review. As I left Revenue Canada shortly after that audit, I have no idea what, if anything, occurred with the actual file.

The following story is *what might have happened in a special investigations audit,* updated to reflect today's technology.

Prologue

Al Edwards sat at his desk reviewing the file in front of him. He had already read his report twice, but he reviewed it once more before dating and signing it. He couldn't believe it; he had spent about one hundred hours auditing the tax returns of an individual—one Harold Gerber—had filed after having been taken to court by the Canada Revenue Agency for failure to file his returns. The individual tax returns—four of them—were obviously made up. He had not been able to confirm any of the information they contained. The companies where Gerber had said he worked; he could find no record of from the source deductions division.

As well, the investments that Gerber claimed to have owned and sold could not be substantiated. A senior auditor had suggested he take a drive by the house where Gerber lived, so he took the family on a drive one Sunday and drove by the house. He had written down the licence plate number of the car in the driveway, a BMW, a model 428i Coupe. He had taken the licence plate number to a Department of Motor Vehicles office and found it was registered to a numbered company. When he interviewed Gerber again, and this time with his boss, Gerber denied it was his signature on the vehicle registration or the purchase agreement, which Edwards had obtained from the car dealership.

After that he went to the insurance company listed on the registration and checked their records, without giving specific details, and found there were four highway tractors also owned by the numbered company. And again, Gerber denied any knowledge of these, noting that he had already told them it wasn't his signature on the registration of the BMW so how could he be involved with a company that also owned the highway tractors?

When asked about who owned the house he got upset. He said it was none of their business! When pressed, he said it was his girlfriend and to leave her out of this. She had her own income and knew nothing about his 'business', which was strange as he denied he had any businesses, or other sources of income for that matter.

As to his tax returns, which he had filed and couldn't substantiate, his opinion was that it was up to the CRA to determine if the reported income was correct. He had been fined for not filing tax returns, so he did. He even had an accountant do the returns for him.

And so, after some one hundred hours of work, his boss had told him to write up the report, along with his comments and observations and request that it be forwarded to the Special Investigations unit for further review. Special Investigations, or SI, had far more resources than did the Individual and Professional group for pursuing taxpayers that were apparently dishonest and who willfully evaded paying income tax.

And that stuck in Edwards' craw—Gerber's tax returns were filed in such a way that he paid the absolute minimum in tax. He had losses from investments he said he had owned that offset, for the most part, any income he claimed from other sources, such as his supposed salary. Of course, he denied having bank accounts or investments so, if that was the case, where did the investment income and losses come from? To that question Gerber had just shrugged.

After one last frustrated look, he applied his signature and put it in his outbox. It was time to move on to the next file. One he hoped would be less frustrating.

PART 1

CHAPTER 1

SIX MONTHS LATER

"Tom, come in here."

"Coming boss," replied the special investigator. Tom walked the few steps to his boss's office. "What's up?"

"Got a file from the Individual and Professional Group that should be right up your alley. Some guy by the name of Gerber didn't file any tax returns. Got taken to court. Filed four years' worth of worthless returns. An auditor there named Edwards spent about a hundred hours trying to verify the reported income and couldn't. But looks like he did some good work. Found a corporation that is also not filing returns that apparently involves Gerber, since the car Gerber is driving turns out to be owned by this company, as do several highway tractors. Gerber denied everything. Said it was up to us to verify his claimed income and the way his tax returns were structured he ended up having to pay very little tax. I want you to go over Edwards' work and come up with a plan of attack. Then we'll review it and try to catch this scumbag."

"Fine by me, boss. You know I like a good challenge!" replied Tom.

He went back to his desk and read through the audit report, then he turned his attention to the attachments. Edwards had been very thorough for a relatively new auditor. He had taken a drive by the scumbag's house and got the licence plate number and make and model of the car in the driveway. He went to the local motor vehicles office and got the details on the registration and found the dealer, which was in Orangeville, and got a copy of the sales invoice. That was where he found it was sold to a numbered company. From the motor vehicle registration, he had learned the name of the insurance agency that issued the insurance policy and through that, had found confirmed the car was registered to the company that owed the four highway tractors that were used to haul the big trailers. Interesting. And, why go to Orangeville to buy a BMW when there was a dealer in Kitchener?

Unfortunately, Edwards had been unable to find any banking information or anything by way of investments held by Gerber. So, where did the money come from to buy the trucks or the car? A business auditor provided information to Edwards about the trucks—after Edwards had tracked them down and requested the file—only to find it was also under review. The business auditor had confirmed that the truck drivers were treated as self-employed contractors and paid by the client company directly, as was the gas for the trucks. All that was paid to the numbered company, suspected to be controlled by Gerber, was the net amount owing on the contract. No copy of that had turned up.

A few of the things Edwards had not done:

1. Called the accountant who prepared the tax returns that Gerber had filed and why did he use an accountant in Oakville;

2. Gone back to the motor vehicle registration office to see if the numbered company owned any other vehicles;

3. Pulled the tax returns of Gerber's girlfriend, who supposedly owned the house; and,

4. Gone to the property registration office and city tax office to confirm she owned the house.

But, from the audit report it appeared that his immediate supervisor suggested that he wrap up the audit, file it as 'no change', but include a recommendation to refer it to Special Investigations for further action. The supervisor had signed off on that recommendation.

So, there it was—Gerber appeared to be a ghost: no confirmed source of income; no confirmed employment; and living with his girlfriend who apparently owned a house in the toney Mulberry area in southeast Kitchener—an area where houses started in the low seven figures and went up.

Thomas reviewed the file again the next day and started to lay out an initial plan for his investigation. First, he would try to get hold of the accountant at the phone number on the return before driving to Oakville. Then he would check with motor vehicles again and also the property registration and property tax departments to see what information they had on the house. He thought about calling the dealership in Orangeville to see if this numbered company had purchased more vehicles from them—but that was down the line. And this early in his investigation the last thing he wanted to do was alert Gerber that Special Investigations had an interest in him. In other words, like Edwards, Thomas's investigation would start as a third-party investigation, hopefully ending in a different outcome from a 'no change' file!

With his plan of attack outlined, he knocked on the wall of his boss's cubical and went in to discuss his initial approach with him.

CHAPTER 2

It was a beautiful spring Monday morning when Tom Thomas headed back into the CRA's office in Kitchener. The sky was blue, the leaves were just starting to come out of bud and the temperature was still a little crisp. He had a spring in his step too as he headed into the office, about the start his investigation of the Gerber file. He was dressed comfortably in golf shirt and slacks with comfortable shoes. He wasn't intending to be out of the office today.

After he got a coffee and settled in at his desk, he called the number of the accountant who had prepared the tax returns…

"World Travel and Tour, may I help you?" said the polite Asian voice.

"Hello? Is this 905-555-2776?"

"Yes, may I help you?" replied the Asian voice.

"Do you have a Giuseppe Risotto there?" enquired Thomas.

"No. This is a travel agency specialized in tours to Asia. Nobody that name work here," the receptionist replied in broken English.

"Could I speak to your supervisor, please? I'm with the Canada Revenue Agency and this is the number I have for an accountant who prepared some tax returns and I need to speak to him."

"No accountant here. But maybe owner know what you talking about. Just minute, please."

"Hello? This is Victoria Wong. I'm the owner. May I help you?"

"Ms. Wong, my name is Tom Thomas—and yes, that is my real name—I'm with the Canada Revenue Agency. I'm looking for a Mr. Giuseppe Risotto. He prepared some tax returns for a person of interest and I wanted to speak to him. Do you know where I can find him?"

"Oh, Mr. Risotto. Yes, I rented him a desk during tax season a few years ago so that he could help my clients file their tax returns. But that was some years ago. Many of our clients are of Asian origin and their English is not so good, so I rented him a desk for maybe five years during tax season to help our clients file their tax returns. But several of my clients complained to me that the Revenue Agency reassessed their returns, disallowing certain expenses—sorry, it was a while ago so I'm not sure which expenses. I tried to contact Mr. Risotto, but the number he had given me as his main contact number had been disconnected and his email address no longer exists. He never came back, and I don't know where he is. Is this about one of my clients?"

"All I can tell you, Ms. Wong, is that the taxpayer I'm calling about isn't Asian. Do you remember a non-Asian male having Mr. Risotto complete a number of tax returns for several different years?"

"We have a number of non-Asian clients, but most don't have us help with their tax returns. But, yes, two years ago we did have a man come in—he wasn't a client—and Mr. Risotto took a few days to complete several tax returns. He told me he didn't trust the guy. The person just gave him some information and told him to complete the returns. He told me that he made sure he stamped the returns stating he had completed the returns only from information provided by the individual. But I don't remember this person's name. And that was the last year Mr. Risotto rented a desk from me."

"Thank you, Ms. Wong. This is very interesting. Can you please give me Mr. Risotto's phone number? I know it's been disconnected, but maybe I can learn something from it. And thank you very much for your help. Oh, one final question, do you know if Mr. Risotto is a member of an accounting association? Did he have initials after his name?"

"No, I don't think he was a member of an association of any kind. He just did the tax returns as a sort of hobby. Something that he had learned doing tax returns for his parents and some friends. And you know, come to think of it, maybe he had another job, as he was here only on Saturdays. He said it was for the convenience of our clients, but maybe there was another reason. His phone number is 519-555-6969 but as I said, it is disconnected."

"Do you still have his email address? I know you said it was no longer valid, but it might help."

After she gave him the email address, Tom said, "Thank you very much, Ms. Wong, you have been a great help."

Tom hung up. *So,* he thought, *why do we have an individual, Gerber, who lives in Kitchener go to Oakville to have his required tax returns completed?* There are a lot of accounting firms, tax preparation companies, even bookkeepers in Waterloo Region. And why would an individual who resides in Southwestern Ontario—for that is all the disconnected phone number told him—go to a travel agency in Oakville to prepare tax returns? He didn't even know if the number was for a landline or a cell phone. And why for a group of people that aren't from his own ethnic background? And what did he do when he filed the returns that resulted in a number of the travel agency's clients being reassessed? Interesting. But he was no further ahead.

The Special Investigations unit had access to other resources that the other units didn't. It had a team of computer specialists who could use the Internet and other technologies to help track companies and individuals and find information that was not normally available to the average person.

***

"Owen, I need your help with trying to track a couple of people," stated Tom.

"What do you need, Tom?" replied Owen Charles, the head of SI's specialized computer team.

"I'm trying to track a couple of people involved in a file I'm working on. The first is a male by the name of Giuseppe Risotto. I tried him at the place where he had his office, a travel agency in Oakville, but he hasn't worked there for a couple of years. They had a phone number for him, 519-555-6969, but it's disconnected. I didn't try a reverse look-up because I already had his name. Maybe you and your team could track down his present contact information. He also has an email address that is no longer valid—grissotto@hotmail.com."

"And the second?" asked Owen Charles.

"Ah, yes, the second. This is a person of interest in the file I'm working on. His name is Harold Gerber. His address is 52 Fig Tree Way in Kitchener. I have a home phone number for him at that address. But what I'd like you to do is see if he has a cell phone and a presence on social media. It's an intriguing case that came from the Individual and Professional audit group. He was taken to court for failure to file tax returns and filed four years' worth. The auditor spent about a hundred hours on the file and could neither prove nor disprove the reported income. But he found some interesting leads that were beyond the group's capabilities so the file was referred to us. Let me know when you find anything."

"Will do, Tom. You know we like a challenge."

Tom went back to his desk. He picked up his phone and dialed the number for the Ontario Ministry of Transportation, a number he kept handy. Once he got the directory, he dialed the extension of his contact there.

"Hi Karen, this is Tom Thomas from the CRA. How are you today?

"That's great, Karen. Listen, I've got a couple of things you can help me with," continued Tom after exchanging pleasantries. "First, I've got a numbered company that owns at least one car, and possible several highway tractors. I'd appreciate it if you could look up the company and do a search to find out exactly how many vehicles it owns, the VIN numbers and the name of the insurance company that carries the liability insurance."

"Good, thanks Karen, here's the number."

"And what's the second thing, Tom?" queried the flirty feminine voice at the other end of the line.

"Can you do a search by registered owner? If I give you a name, can you tell me if they own any vehicles?"

"Ummm, sure, it might help if you can narrow down the search to a city or region, otherwise we're going through all of Ontario."

"OK, the area I'm looking at initially is the Region of Waterloo and I've got one name for now: Harold Gerber, the last name is spelled G-E-R-B-E-R." Tom also gave her the details on the numbered company.

"Got it, Tom."

"I can come by and pick up the info. When do you think you'll have it?"

"Better give me a couple of days. I'll call you Wednesday. OK?"

"Great, talk to you then." He hung up the phone and turned to his computer. Might not hurt if he did some looking through the Internet as well to see what he could find out about the mysterious Mr. Gerber.

As he left for the evening, he stuck his head into his boss's cubicle to let him know he was stopping at the land registry and property tax offices on his way in the next morning to check out the house's ownership.

CHAPTER 3

The next morning, Tuesday, he arrived at the Land Registry office just after it opened. It wasn't busy yet and he managed to get to a clerk almost immediately. The middle-aged, overweight woman with dyed hair that looked orange, but probably should have been red, wobbled up to the counter and studied his identification and looked at his face a couple of times and then asked what she could do for him. He told her he would like the land registry records for 52 Fig Tree Way, Kitchener. And yes, he would like the whole history, not just the current year please. The woman tapped out the address on her computer and then hit the print button. She informed him that only the past ten years were digitized, and she'd have go into the stacks if he really wanted the previous five years, going back to when the house was built. Thomas confirmed that, yes, he would like the hard copy files as well. She gave him a look and shuffled off.

She returned about twenty minutes later and handed the file to him, telling him he could photocopy it on the pay copier against the far wall or make notes, but he wasn't allowed to leave with them. She also handed him the printouts of the last ten years of land registry records. Tom said thank you and carried the files over to a table. He leafed through the hard copy files. He pulled his cell phone from his pocket and photographed the pages one by one. Not all appeared relevant, but he liked to be thorough. When he was finished, he took the hard copies back to the clerk and, giving her a wide smile, thanked her very much for her help. She smiled back and placed the files into a tray to be refiled when she had a moment.

Next, he headed to the Property Tax office, which was a couple of blocks away. When he got there, he asked if the taxes were paid by cheque or by electronic transfer. The cute young clerk checked and told him they were paid monthly by electronic transfer. He asked if he could get a copy of that information. She was unsure, asked him to wait a minute, and went to get her manager. The manager asked to see his identification and repeated the request to make sure he understood it. Tom confirmed he did. The manager then said banking information was confidential and so Tom would have to produce a Demand for Information, which for audit purposes had the same effect as a search warrant. And, like a search warrant he would have to prove to his superiors that the information was instrumental to his investigation.

The manager, however, was able to provide him with the amount of property taxes paid on the Fig Tree Way house for the past three years.

Tom thanked the manager.

He stopped at a Tim Hortons and got a large black dark roast coffee and an apple fritter. He sat a table and flipped through the information from the land registry office. The house had been built fifteen years ago. It had changed hands twice, both times doubling in price, with the latest sale being three years ago to one Jacqueline Mendes for the price of $1.2 million. According to the record, a mortgage was held by the Overland Bank and Trust Company. He looked at the property tax records and found the taxes were $4,552 for the previous year. The taxes were being paid monthly.

Once back at the office, he hung up his jacket, loosened his tie and sat down at his desk and started to update his findings. He then updated his boss and told him about the Demand for Information request from the Property Tax Office. He now knew what bank Ms. Mendes used, so maybe that might be an avenue of investigation. However, since the house was owned by Ms. Mendes and they didn't know her relationship to Gerber, the boss didn't think they had enough to request a Demand. But now that they knew the owner's name, he recommended Tom request her tax return and see what sources of income she had to justify the purchase of a $1.2 million house.

On leaving his boss's office, he called Records and asked for Mendes' tax returns for the past four years. He had an address and postal code but sorry, no social insurance number.

Then he booted up his computer and checked his email. There were myriad administrative emails, but one in particular stood out. It was from Owen Charles. He opened it and read through it, and then re-read it. The outcome of the Internet and computer database searches had turned up no information on Harold Gerber whatsoever. It was like he was a ghost, or someone who lived twenty years in the past. No digital footprint. No mention of him in any searches. No profile. No employment history. No chat room activity. Nothing.

Tom shook his head and hit reply. He said he was amazed, but then asked Owen to do a similar search on a Jacqueline Mendes. He gave as his rationale that she owned the house that Gerber gave as his address and he used her phone number as his contact. Tom provided the computer sleuth with her address and telephone number, as well as the name of her bank and asked Owen to do a detailed search and get back to him when he had something. Or if he didn't.

★★★

Mid-Wednesday morning he got a call from Karen at the Ontario Ministry of Transportation.

"Tom, I've found something you need to take a look at, but I think it would be better if you came over here so we can go over it in detail," Karen told him.

"That good, or that bad?"

"Well, you gave me the name of a numbered company and the VINs of several vehicles registered to it. There are a lot more. And I'd rather go over it here than fax or send you PDFs of the registrations."

"OK, give me an hour. How about I bring in some Chinese? Sounds like I owe you!"

"Sounds good, but nothing with hot chillies or peppers."

An hour and a bit later Tom parked in the guest parking at the Ministry, told the guard who he was seeing and signed in.

"So, what have you got, Karen?" Tom queried as he entered her office.

"First, let me see what you got. Umm, noodles, sesame chicken, vegetables and beef. Fairly healthy." As she started to make up a plate and take a pop she continued, "Well, I tracked both the vehicles owned by the numbered company as well as looking for vehicles owned by Harold Gerber. I found that the numbered company, in addition to the highway tractors we already know about, owns a half-dozen more. The highway tractors had all been purchased ten years earlier. What was interesting was that the trucks had been bought in twos and threes from different dealers all over southwestern Ontario. And Gerber wasn't the only one who had purchased the trucks; a couple were bought by a woman, Jacqueline Mendes. And in addition to the highway tractors, the numbered company also owns two Mercedes vans, three SUVs and a couple of cars. The insurance policies are scattered among several property and casualty companies. If all the vehicles were insured by one company, a fleet policy, there would normally be a bit of a discount. But by using several companies it seemed the intention was to reduce the chance all the vehicles could be traced back to one owner."

Tom thanked Karen and after they finished lunch, he headed back to the office to update his boss on the progress of the investigation, His boss agreed there was an obvious attempt by Gerber to obfuscate his business activity. Whether this was simply a matter of tax evasion or some wider form of criminal activity was yet to be determined. His boss asked Tom to make up a memo of what he knew so far since it sounded like more work was needed before they talked to Gerber and Mendes.

CHAPTER 4

Sunday turned to a bright sunny day and Tom asked his wife Lisa, if she was interested in going for a drive.

"Sure, where to?" she asked.

"I thought we might drive down through the Mulberry neighbourhood, and then go for an ice cream at that shop you like over towards Stratford."

"Hmm, a drive through the southeast part of town before heading west? What are you up to, Tom?"

"I've got this file I'm working on and I thought I'd take a page from the original auditor and go check out where the individual in question calls home. Won't take long. Promise."

Early in the afternoon Tom and his wife were driving through the tony Mulberry area, going slowly, looking at the various mansions and pretending to pay attention to several. As they passed 52 Fig Tree Way Tom slowed and notice three vehicles in the driveway. Two were cars, but one was a black Mercedes van with a logo on the side: A golden helmet, with the name Mambrino underneath and the words wrapped around the top of the helmet in italics 'Discretion Assured'. All the lettering was in gold. Interesting.

Of particular interest was the For Sale on the front lawn, with a notice on the top 'Coming Soon'. He quickly took a few pictures with his cell phone, making sure to get the licence plates in the pictures as well as the For-Sale sign and the name of the agent. If anyone came out and asked what he was doing, he could simply say he and his wife were interested and he was taking pictures of the house and the agent's name.

★★★

Monday, back in the office he checked his emails and saw one from Owen Charles. He had found that Jacqueline Mendes did have a presence of social media, including an email address and other social media accounts. While she had these, she didn't seem to be overly active, mostly following news stories and a few celebrities as well as friends and exchanging pics, birthday greetings, etc. Nothing exciting or leading in terms of the numbered company.

Another email contained the PDFs of her tax returns for the past four years. But before looking at those though, he told his boss about the Sunday drive and finding a van with the logo as well as the fact the house was going up for sale. His boss suggested calling the sales agent and asking the price of the house as well as whether if there was going to be an open house. Tom agreed and went back to his cubicle and made the call.

His boss reminded him he needed an email outlining where the audit stood.

CHAPTER 5

After Tom phoned the RE/MAX office and spoke to the listing agent, he prepared an email to his boss about what he knew, and didn't know, so far.

What we know:

1. The listed company owns at least ten highway tractors, three vans and two cars.

2. It appears to operate under the name 'Mambrino' and its logo is a golden helmet with the words 'Discretion Assured' in italics around it. This is based on my seeing a van with this logo on it, painted black, in Jacqueline Mendes' driveway Sunday last by myself and my wife. Subsequent investigation confirmed the van was one of the known three owned by the numbered company.

3. The vehicles are insured through various property and casualty companies.

4. Two of the known vehicles were signed for by Jacqueline Mendes.

5. Harold Gerber has no social media profile and we have been unable to find any banking or other financial information.

6. Mendes owns a house located at 52 Fig Tree Way, Kitchener. According to land registry records she bought the house three years ago for $1.2 million. The mortgage is held by the Overland Bank and Trust Company. The mortgage and property taxes are paid by automatic withdrawal from a bank account with the same financial institution.

7. The house is currently up for sale. According to the listing agent, the house will be on the market within the next week at a price of $1.8 million and there will be an open house on a weekend, two weeks from now. (I used my personal phone and expressed interest in seeing it during the open house so the agent doesn't know I'm with the CRA.)

8. I took at quick look at the Mendes woman's tax returns. Last year, she reported that she is self-employed as a Financial Consultant and reported gross income of $200,000 and a net of $182,500. She claimed a portion of her home as an office and deducted portions of her house expenses, but not depreciation.

9. What we don't know:

1. So far, the tech folks have been unable to trace the 'accountant', Giuseppe Risotto, after he stopped working at the travel agency in Oakville (need to follow-up).

2. What the numbered company does to earn income, other than for the three tractors we know are used by the company that was audited by the large business group. We know it owns several other highway tractors and cars and vans. Where are they and what are they being used for?

3. The Mendes woman's clients or client to generate the reported income.

4. As previously noted, any financial information about Gerber.

5. The relationship between Mendes and Gerber. Is it purely business, e.g., she has provided him with a mailing address? Are they living common-law or are they married? Why she signed the purchase agreement for two of the vehicles, one a car, one a van. She must be involved in the company, but how?

After reviewing the email, he hit send and went back to looking at the Mendes woman's tax returns. They looked relatively straightforward, she had paid both parts of CPP—the employer and employee portion. She contributed the maximum allowable to an RRSP and to a Tax Free Savings Account. She did not claim a married or common-law relationship. The e-file was just the tax return. He would have to request the hard copy to get the source documents—the businesses financial statements and receipts for the RRSP contributions. This he did.

Just as he finished, his boss knocked on his cubical wall. "Tom, I think we need to go see the director to discuss what you've got so far. I'm concerned about the sale of the house. If they move, we might lose track of them—at least until she files a change of address with us or files next year's tax return—assuming she does. I've called his office, and he's expecting us. Come on."

They were at the director's office a couple of minutes later, after a short elevator ride. "Hi, Margaret," greeted Tom's boss.

"Go on in, he's expecting you," replied the administrative assistant.

"Hi, Bob" said Tom's boss. "Tom, I don't think you've met Bob Hamilton before. Bob, this is Tom Thomas, one of my best investigators."

The two exchanged pleasantries then got down to business. After reviewing the notes Tom had made and the fact that the supposed girlfriend, Jacqueline Mendes, had reported a gross income of $200,000 and appeared to have signed the purchase agreement for two of the vehicles owned by the numbered company, as well as the pending sale of her house, Bob Hamilton agreed that they needed to move a little quicker. He asked who the original auditor on the file was and Tom told him. The director thought that Edwards might want to be back on the case.

He said, "I think it might raise suspicions, Tom, if you were the initial auditor of the Mendes woman's file. You discovered she signed for two of the vehicles, a car and a van, that are owned by the numbered company, which appears to be operating under this Mambrino name. So, let's get Edwards to audit her return. I'll give his boss a call and have him seconded to the investigation. I want you to go to the open house. If Gerber isn't reporting income and you can't find a bank account, maybe he is 'investing' the money in other ways... like antiques or collectibles. I'll call the London office and ask them to lend us a female appraiser. When the open house happens, I want the two of you to go look at it and she can see if it looks like there are collectibles there."

"Sounds good," said Tom.

"Do we know the addresses of this supposed Mambrino company?" asked Hamilton.

"I haven't checked all the addresses—the numbered company, which I assume is operating as Mambrino, has given three addresses, depending on where the various vehicles were purchased. I know the one in Kitchener is in the middle of the Grand River, so I assume the others are fake, but I'll check them out," replied Tom.

"Good, and let's send copies of Gerber's handwriting from his signature on his tax return and on the sales agreements to the RCMP's handwriting analysis unit to confirm that the two are indeed the same. I'll also authorize a Demand for Information for both the bank and the Property Tax office so we can see who owns those accounts and if Gerber also has an account," stated the director. He continued, "So, to summarize, we have a two-pronged approach. Edwards will audit the Mendes woman. Tom, you will go ahead with the Demands at the Bank and Property Tax office as well as go to the open house with the appraiser. I'll arrange a contact for you in the London office." With that, the meeting ended as the director picked up the phone to call Edwards' boss.

***

After lunch, Thomas and Edwards met to go over the plan. Edwards was very happy to be involved again as this case had stuck in his craw—the fact he had spent a hundred hours and had not been able to verify any of the reported income irked him still. They agreed that since the Mendes woman claimed her home as her place of business it would be better for Edwards to call her and arrange a time for her to bring in her invoices and expense receipts for him to review in the office, as opposed to working in her house, which might tip off Gerber, who had met him previously.

With that out of the way, Tom, turned to Google Maps to check the addresses of the other two locations given on the purchase and vehicle registration documents. As anticipated, the one in New Hamburg was located in the Nith River and the other one was located in a soccer park in London. Tom then emailed Owen Charles and asked if he had had an opportunity to look for Giuseppe Risotto.

While he awaited the Demands for Information, he reviewed what he knew about the Gerber file and this Mambrino company, with the golden helmet logo. He checked Wikipedia and found out that Mambrino was a fictional Moorish king. According to some poems about this supposed king, the helmet was made 'of pure gold and rendered its wearer invulnerable'. *Interesting,* he thought.

CHAPTER 6

Friday morning, Al Edwards finished reviewing the Mendes' tax returns and then picked up his desk phone and dialed the number on the tax return. "Hello," answered a pleasant female voice.

"Ms. Mendes?"

"Yes."

"Ms. Mendes, my name is Al Edwards and I'm an auditor with the Kitchener Tax Services office. Your tax returns for the past two years were selected for a random review. I understand that you work from home, is that correct?" asked Edwards.

"Yes, I work out of my home. Is that a problem?" responded Mendes.

"No, not at all. But because you work from home, I think it might be easier if you could bring all your records for the last two years to our office. I'll need invoices, expense receipts, how you calculated the portion of your home expense, purchases, as well as your business and personal bank account statements for the same period. I know that's a lot of material, so why don't you take the weekend to get everything together and then come to our office on Frederick Street at 10:00 a.m. next Monday morning. You have to buzz, but I'll be down at the main entrance to meet you. I just think it would be less obtrusive if you brought your records here. I can review everything and then, if

I have any questions, we can meet to discuss them. Will that work for you?"

"I probably don't need that long, Mr. Edwards. I keep very good records and everything is filed by year with a copy of my tax return. But yes, that's very kind of you to give me a few days to make sure I have everything together, so yes, I'll have a couple of boxes with my files at your office on Monday at ten. Would you be able to help me carry them in from the car?

"That's not a problem. I'll see you Monday at 10:00 a.m." replied Edwards and then hung up the phone. *Good,* he thought, *I can check the licence plate number of her car on Monday and see if it corresponds to the car she purchased for the Mambrino company.*

★★★

The same morning Tom Thomas got a phone call. "Hello, Mr. Thomas?"

"Yes?" replied Tom.

"Mr. Thomas, this is Sandra McLean from the London office. I understand you may need my services."

"Oh, hello—please call me Tom. Yes, did you get the details about what we are planning?"

"Only that you may need an appraiser to go to an open house, but I don't know why," responded Sandra McLean.

"Well, we have an individual who is under investigation because the source of his income can't be verified. We've discovered a numbered company that owns several vehicles, including highway tractors, which isn't filing tax returns. We haven't been able to track down any bank accounts or investments. He lives in a house with his girlfriend, or we think she is his girlfriend, and the house is going up for sale. One thought is that perhaps any profits from this company are being invested in antiques that he bought for cash. Or maybe he's helping to pay the mortgage on the house. We'd like you to pose as my wife, and we'll go to the open house. I'll try to find out why the girlfriend—a lady by the name of Jacqueline Mendes—is selling and if the agent knows where she is moving while you take a close look through the house to see if there is anything of value, which might tell us where the money is going," explained Tom.

"You say the girlfriend owns the house. How do you know she didn't purchase the house and antiques, if there are any, herself?" asked McLean.

"We don't. But we know she has a mortgage with a local bank, and she is the owner of the house, according to the Land Registry and Property Tax offices here. One of our Individual and Professional group's auditors is currently auditing her returns for the past two years. Her returns state that she is a self-employed financial consultant who works from home. So, we're covering her off. And I'm waiting on Demands to take to the Property Tax office and to her bank to get the bank account information from which the taxes are being paid, and one for the bank to find out whose account that is and if she has other investments there. Then we'll compare that to what the auditor who is auditing her returns finds. But the potential sale of the house is a concern because if she sells with a quick closing, we may not be able to find either our ghost corporation or its owner again," detailed Thomas.

"So, who's your target?" asked McLean.

"We have the original taxpayer, a man by the name of Gerber, who was taken to court several years ago for failing to file tax returns and then filed four years' worth with apparently made-up numbers. So, he's the target. In addition, we have the ghost company, which apparently goes by the name Mambrino that owns a number of highway tractors and other vehicles—SUVs and cars—which also isn't filing returns," explained Tom.

"Do you have an address for the company or is that fake too?"

"The addresses used on the purchase agreements and vehicle registrations are fake. Three are different addresses depending on where the vehicles were purchased. Two are in the middle of rivers and one is the soccer fields beside the London Psychiatric Hospital."

"Huh, interesting file. Give me a couple of days' notice, if you can, about the open house. Do you want to go on the Saturday or Sunday?"

"Which is best for you?"

"The Saturday, probably. Any idea when?"

"I called the agent and she agreed to call me back to let me know. My wife and I found out it was coming on the market when we went for a 'Sunday drive' a week ago. I called the agent on my personal cell phone, so she doesn't know I work for the CRA."

"Quite the cloak and dagger of you," chuckled McLean. "OK, give me a call when you know."

After Tom hung up, he made some notes of the conversation and then checked his email. Finally, Owen Charles had found the elusive Mr. Risotto. He had moved and hadn't, as yet, filed a change of address with either the CRA or the Ministry of Transportation. He now lived in the lovely town of Goderich. And, from what Charles had found out checking source deduction records for all of the companies located there (*No wonder it took so long,* thought Tom), it seems that Mr. Risotto was working at the marina. In what capacity it wasn't known, but it seems he had been there for about six months. Owen had been able to find a phone number and address for him. That was good, but Tom wasn't about to drive to Goderich to interview Risotto on speculation. He'd wait and see how the audit progressed first and then he might call him to just ask about the tax returns he had prepared for Gerber. But that could wait for now. He replied to the email, thanking the computer sleuth for tracking Risotto down.

The following Monday, the two Demands came through. Tom decided to wait until Tuesday to serve the one on the Property Tax office and then go to the bank later in the week, after Edwards had the information from Mendes and Tom knew which bank accounts she said she had.

CHAPTER 7

Promptly at ten the following Monday morning Jacqueline Mendes rang the bell at the CRA's Frederick Street office. Al Edwards had been waiting for her and opened the door, said hello, and identified himself. He hoped she didn't place his name with the auditor who had audited the Gerber file. Certainly, she had not seen him before, but he didn't know what Gerber might have told her. She said she had several boxes in the trunk of her car and Edwards pointed to the trolley he had with him. She held the door as he wheeled it out and down the ramp as he followed her to her car. He made a mental note of the licence number, make, and model as he unloaded three bankers' boxes of files from the car.

She was definitely a good-looking lady, slender, with long dark hair in a ponytail and wearing slacks and blouse with running shoes.

Jacqueline Mendes opened the lid of each and explained what was in it: two held invoices and expense by year, including total expenses for things like hydro, natural gas, and mortgage interest as well as detailed expenses pertaining to the business. Attached to the returns were copies of RRSP receipts and tax slips for investment income. The third contained bank statements, organized by year.

Edwards was quite impressed with the organization of the files and told her so. He thanked her and told her he would be in touch after he had gone through everything. He advised her he also had other files he was working on and so not to be too concerned if he didn't get back to her for a few weeks. He assured her it was simply a routine review—that they tried to review all self-employed people every few years and since this was her first review, she shouldn't be too concerned.

***

At about the same time as Edwards was receiving the files from Jacqueline Mendes, Tom Thomas was presenting the Demand for Information to the supervisor of Kitchener's Property Tax Office. After reviewing it, the supervisor took Thomas into an office and asked him to please wait while he retrieved the information regarding the bank account information regarding the property taxes. He returned in a few minutes with a printout showing the account details at the Overland Bank and Trust Company from which the taxes were paid monthly by automatic withdrawal. The signature on the authorization was that of Ms. Mendes. Tom wasn't really surprised. He thanked the supervisor for his cooperation and reminded him, again, that the CRA's enquiries were confidential and if he told the property owner about the enquiry, he may be subject to prosecution. And he also reminded him that there may be nothing resulting from the information the CRA obtained, it was simply part of an ongoing investigation, which may or may not result in any charges against the taxpayer.

When Tom got back into the office, he emailed Edwards and asked if the bank account information he had from Mendes matched the bank account information he got from the Property Tax office. It did. Edwards indicated he had found a separate bank account, a business account, which she used to deposit her income and pay the direct expenses. He indicated he'd keep Thomas apprised of his progress.

Tom then turned his attention back to Gerber. From the vehicle registration information, he knew that the vehicles of the numbered, or 'ghost' company as they were calling it now—which he now presumed was operating as Mambrino—had the trucks and cars insured with three separate insurers. The first, which the business auditor had discovered and insured four highway tractors, was TransNational Insurance Ltd., which was headquartered in Toronto. This company also insured other trucks and assets that were owned by the client company, which paid all the operating expenses, and only paid a net amount to Mambrino, although that was not the name on the cheques. Instead, the cheques were made out to a numbered company.

Another insurer, AllRisk, insured the cars and panel vans, and a third, Centrina, insured the other six highway tractors.

Tom checked Google and found that AllRisk's head office was located in Mississauga, but there was a local agent in Cambridge. Tom entered the information in his phone for both then turned his attention to Centrina. Centrina turned out to be a relatively small insurer with its head office in Barrie. *Why Barrie?* Tom thought.

The next morning, Tom sent off an original vehicle purchase agreement, along with a copy of the phony tax returns Gerber had previously filed to the RCMP's handwriting analysis unit. He then turned his attention back to the file and pondered how to find out where the other highway tractors were employed, as well as the SUVs and vans. He decided he'd try contacting the AllRisk insurance agent in Cambridge and see what he could learn.

The agent in the Cambridge office, one John McGuire, declined to provide any information over the phone as he was uncertain if the call was another CRA scam call trying to learn information about a client that could be used for profit, however he did agree to meet with Tom at ten the following morning at his office.

Just after Tom hung up the phone his personal cell phone rang. It was the RE/MAX agent handling the sale of the Mendes woman's house. She told him that an open house was scheduled for both the Saturday and Sunday of the following weekend. Tom thanked her and said he and his wife would probably be there.

He then called Sandra McLean, the appraiser in the London office. "Hello, Sandra?"

"Yes?"

"It's Tom Thomas from the Kitchener office. The open house is next weekend. Which day is best for you?"

"Oh hello, Tom. Ahh, valuation issue, right? Looking for collectables?"

"That's right, Sandra."

"I think Saturday would be best. What time?"

"The open house is from two to four. Do you want to meet for lunch first?"

"Sure, sounds good. That way we can plan a course of action and maybe take a drive by first."

"OK, how about meeting at Kelsey's on old King Street. It's just north of the 401 and only a short drive to her house. We can leave your car there and go together."

"Sounds good. See you there about 12:30 p.m.?"

"Sure, looking forward to meeting you. Oh, by the way, how will I recognize you?"

"I've got short dark hair and I'll be wearing glasses and a red jacket. You?"

"I've got a beard and blondish red hair. Not sure of my outfit, but we'll find each other."

After Tom got off the phone, he walked over to his boss's cubicle to give him an update.

***

The following morning, Tom left home a little later than normal as he had decided to go to meet the insurance agent in Cambridge before going into the office, so he had time for a decent breakfast, during which he brought his wife up to date on his plans for the Saturday afternoon of the weekend after next.

Just before ten the next morning, Tom drove into the parking lot of John McGuire Insurance Associates Ltd., which was located in the Hespler area of Cambridge. Tom went into the office and asked the receptionist for John McGuire.

"Mr. McGuire," Tom said, as he showed him his Special Investigator identification. McGuire was sixtyish and the perfect picture of an insurance agent: somewhat rotund, with pinstripe suit pants, suspenders, and a bow tie.

"Yes," replied the insurance agent. "Wow, Special Investigations, eh? Haven't had one of you boys visit me before."

"You've had the pleasure of meeting other auditors from the CRA?" queried Tom.

"Only a couple of times—both times looking to confirm ownership of cars or businesses," replied McGuire. "What can I help you with?"

"Perhaps we should step into your office so we're not in so public a place to talk?"

"Oh, that's all right. Sally here has heard it all and besides, she'll have to look up the information. I'm helpless when it comes to computers." Sally was in her fifties wearing lipstick that was a little too red, the dyed hair more yellowish than blonde and the dress perhaps a size too small. *Interesting pair,* thought Tom.

"All right, he gave Sally the VIN numbers for two cars and three panel vans registered to Mambrino. Can you confirm the ownership and if any of these vehicles are leased to another company? I assume there would be some sort of rider on the policy indicating the user."

"Just a minute," replied the receptionist. "Ahhh, yeeessss—the system shows that one car has a J. Mendes listed as the primary driver—the other car is just showing it is a company vehicle, meaning any employee can use it—and—three panel vans… they are leased to a courier service. Mambrino Same Day Courier—it's a subsidiary of Mambrino," Sally stated as she slowly worked through the details.

"Do you have details on the courier service?" asked Tom, trying not to look too enthusiastic.

"Yes, the address is shown as 2244 Cedar Street in Tillsonburg."

"Any other information?"

"The courier service indicates its area of operations as South Central Ontario, which would mean—let me see the geographic area. OK, essentially Dufferin County across through Wellington and Huron Counties, Middlesex, Oxford, and up through Waterloo Region."

"That's very detailed. Why do you need that level of detail?" asked Tom.

McGuire responded, "We need to know the geographic area to determine the insurance rate. For instance, if the client was driving regularly to Toronto, the rate would be higher because the probability of accidents is higher. The same if the client were regularly going into the United States, say regularly to Detroit or to New York."

"What happens if the client doesn't stick to the insured area and has an accident?"

"That depends," responded McGuire. "If we determine—and by we, I mean the insurance company—that it was more or less a one off—not regular business, then we'd pay the claim. But if turns out that the client was 'mistaken' (McGuire making quotes with his fingers.) about the area of operations and they regularly operated in a higher risk location, then the insurer may well decline the claim. And we explain this, especially to business customers, at the time the policy is issued, and we also send them a letter on the renewal of the policy confirming the operating area and asking them to update any changes that might have been made to their business operations."

"Oh, by the way, which company pays the insurance premiums, the parent company or the courier company?"

"The courier company," replied Sally, after a quick look at her screen.

"Thank you, Mr. McGuire, and you too, Sally," he said, giving the dyed yellowish-haired receptionist a wink and a nod. "If you could print that information for me, Sally, I'll be on my way. And I must remind both of you that any enquiry by the Canada Revenue Agency is confidential and any information about my visit or the information I requested is confidential. Failure to comply may result in prosecution. Is that understood?

Sally printed out the information of the various vehicles and both she and McGuire confirmed they understood and would not advise the clients of the CRA's interest in them.

Tom then said thank you and left. He drove to a nearby Tim Hortons and went in and bought a dark roast, black, and sat and perused the documents he had obtained.

When he got back to the office, he knocked on his boss's cubical and told him what he'd learned. He suggested getting the tax return for the courier company and checking it out. His boss said he had enough on his plate. He would phone the chief of SI in the London Tax Service office and give him the information Tom had discovered and ask him to arrange to get both the payroll records and tax returns to review, assuming the courier company had actually filed any!

CHAPTER 8

Saturday arrived and found Tom and his wife, Lisa, grocery shopping in the morning. Later in the morning, Tom changed into what he thought would be appropriate for a couple going to an open house—jeans, sports shirt, and a jacket. He went to meet Sandra McLean for lunch. She was a woman in her mid-forties, so they didn't look mismatched as a couple. And like Tom, she was wearing casual attire—slacks with a shirt and scarf. There they discussed the purpose of the visit again.

Not wanting to look too anxious, the pair arrived at the 52 Fig Tree Way just after two-thirty. Sandra and he walked around the house casually at first, then they separated and Sandra started another circuit, this time paying more attention to the furnishings and paintings on the walls, meanwhile Tom chatted up the sales representative. He asked her why the owner had decided to sell. The agent told him that the owners were looking to move farther out of the city, perhaps to New Hamburg or Stratford. She had referred them to a couple of colleagues who knew those areas better than she did. As she understood it, the wife—for that is what she thought she was—worked as a consultant and had clients over most of southwestern Ontario and the husband—for that is what she thought he was—had diverse business interests in the same area, so it really mattered little as to where they lived. But they wanted more land.

Tom ventured to ask, "So if they are married, why is the house only listed in her name?"

The agent told him, "That's not that uncommon when one of the two has significant business interests. They want to protect the higher earner in the case of bankruptcy or a lawsuit from having their house lost in any legal action. And in this case, since the wife had her own significant income it was not unreasonable to assume that she had the financial resources to pay the mortgage and other costs associated with running the home."

Tom thanked her—he wanted to ask who the agents were in New Hamburg and Stratford but didn't want to push his luck. He found Sandra looking carefully at an old rolltop desk and at the oil painting above it. "These are very interesting," Sandra said, as he came up beside her.

"Why?" asked Tom.

"Well, this desk is very old—I'd think eighteenth century—and it is made without nails—dowels hold it together and tongue and grove joints. I'd have to do some checking, but I expect it is from around the time of the American Revolution and probably worth about $15,000, given the excellent shape it's in. In addition, there are some very nice old oil and watercolour paintings on the walls. I'd have to take pictures of some of the other artwork and look at books and contact appraisers, but there is a lot of money hanging on these walls, Tom."

"Do you think you can snap off a couple of shots with your camera phone?"

"I'll try, but you try to cover me as I don't want to look too interested in the artwork."

Sandra managed to get a couple of pics and as she was leaving told the agent, "Such a lovely house. They have some beautiful things. I'm with a charity that raises money by hosting house and garden tours, and I'm sure many people would like to tour a house like this. It's too bad they are moving."

The agent said, "Well, they aren't going far—maybe New Hamburg or Stratford if that isn't too far. I can give you the agents' names that are helping them there and once they settle you could contact them."

"Oh, that would be wonderful," gushed Sandra as she wrote the names and phone numbers in her notepad application on her smart phone.

After they left, Sandra sent Tom the names and phone numbers to his email address. They headed to a Williams Coffee Pub and over a cappuccino they discussed what they'd learned. It was clear that while the Mendes woman's income could cover the mortgage and house costs, there was no way it could cover the cost of the collectables in the place. That must be Gerber's contribution and it was a good way to launder illegally gotten gains—the income from the company Tom assumed he controlled. Tom thanked Sandra for her help and she told him she would follow up on valuation issues around the paintings she had taken pictures of and get back to him within the next couple of weeks. It would take time to have qualified appraisers look at the photos, but she was confident that there were several hundred thousand dollars of artwork and collectables in the house. He dropped her back at the Kelsey's, where she had left her car, and headed home.

***

When Tom got home, he got on his computer and, while the latest events were still fresh in his mind drafted an email to himself at work and copied his boss. His wife asked how the visit went—her curiosity raised because Tom took a woman, an appraiser, from the London office with him instead of her. Tom simply told her that it was interesting and that there was definitely something amiss. Without going into detail, he told her that there were valuables in the house that couldn't be explained by the declared income of the woman who owned the house. That and the fact that the real estate agent was under the impression that the 'husband' also had a source of business income.

"Sounds like you've got a live one," stated Lisa, as she poured them each a glass of white wine.

CHAPTER 9

Come Monday morning, Tom met with his boss again and brought him up to speed in more detail than was in his email. They talked about his meeting with the insurance agent in Cambridge and the discovery of the courier service in Tillsonburg. With respect to the tractors insured by TransNational, the information contained in the previous audit indicated that a business auditor had verified that the company that was leasing the tractors was paying the insurance and the drivers and just sending a net lease payment to Mambrino. But they didn't have an address, so Tom would follow up with the business auditor to see if he had that information, if not, he would have to go back to the company. And finally, as to the insurance company in Barrie, Centrina, they decided Tom would phone and ask nicely for the insurance documents and if they declined to provide them, the boss would authorize a Demand for Information and Tom would deliver it personally, accompanied by a member of the RCMP!

When Tom got back to his desk, he checked his email and saw a message from Al Edwards.

Got something interesting. She included some financial statements and bank accounts not related to her business. The bank information is from a separate bank—one in New York City—and the financial statements relate to a company called Mambrino. Not really financial statements as such, but a list of payments and sources. When can we get together? Tom was more than a little excited. He replied, "How about 1:00 p.m., just after lunch?"

Al responded that was fine; he'd bring the file with him.

Tom then forward Al's email to his boss and the time of the meeting and asked if he wanted to sit in.

He did.

CHAPTER 10

At one o'clock in the afternoon the three met in an interview room in the SI offices. Al laid out what he had found so far. Insofar as the Mendes woman's business was concerned, he had found very little to be concerned about. But, and it was a big but, he had found in her records a few documents unrelated to her business: one, a monthly bank statement from eighteen months ago from the First State Bank of New York, in New York City, that showed two bi-weekly bank deposits of $6,500 and $9,250. The opening balance was $255,250 and the closing balance was $271,000. As well, there was a handwritten sheet with amounts listed, but those amounts didn't relate to her financial consulting business. This had been determined by looking at invoices as well as her deposits to her known business account. The total of those amounts was $1.2 million. However, there were no dates on the paper. Second—a copy of her personal charge account statement for the previous October that was misfiled in her business account files. Of interest was a charge for two return tickets to New York City with Porter Airlines. It also included a hotel charge for a Holiday Inn overnight stay.

All of them agreed this was very interesting. It was obvious that the money in the New York bank must come from the unreported income of Mambrino, but what may be obvious still needs to be proved. Could they crack the Mendes woman? Should they approach Gerber and see if he comes clean? It was decided it was too risky to do the former and to do the latter too early might give Gerber time to sell the trucks and move out of the country.

What to do?

The boss said it was time to talk to Bob Hamilton again.

When they got to the director's office, Tom's boss told his secretary it was important that they see the director right away. She went to the office door and then motioned them to go on in.

"What's up?" queried the director.

Tom's boss introduced Al Edwards to the director and then said "Bob, young Al here has found a couple of interesting things in the Mendes woman's file."

"Oh yes, that's right—the Gerber investigation and we decided to have Al audit the Mendes woman's file as she owned the house he gave as his address," the director remembered. "What did you find, Al, that got everyone so excited?"

Edwards replied, clearing his throat "Ah, well sir—the audit itself was clean, but in the documents she gave me were three of interest: first, a monthly bank statement from a New York City bank showing a couple of deposits and a balance of $271,000; second, a charge card statement, not one she uses for business, that includes a charge for a Porter Airlines return ticket to New York coinciding with the date of a deposit; and lastly, a slip of paper with numbers on it that total $1.2 million. Nothing in her business or personal accounts would justify that amount of money."

"Well, that certainly is interesting!" exuberated the director, rubbing his hands together. "What's next?"

Tom's boss said, "Well Bob, that's why we're here. There are a few avenues we can explore. Oh, and I should also say that the amounts that Al has found help substantiate something Tom found out when he went to an open house at the Mendes house with an appraiser from the London office. Tom?"

"Thanks, boss. According to the appraiser, she thinks there is a lot of money in collectibles in the house. How much? She's not sure. She took notes and some pics with her smartphone. She is going to go through some research material and get back to me, but the furnishings and collectables are probably worth several hundred thousand dollars to quote her 'there is a lot of money hanging on these walls.' What Al found helps substantiate her opinion."

"And where are you in your investigation?" asked the director.

"Still third party only," replied Tom, continuing, "I found a courier company in Tillsonburg that uses the panel vans and one of the cars Gerber bought. It's called 'Mambrino Same Day Courier' and has four employees. Its area of operation is South Central Ontario. We still need to talk to another insurance company in Barrie that insures six of the tractors."

Tom's boss interrupted, "I called the head of SI in London to see if they can see if it is filing corporate and payroll returns. I didn't want Tom running all over Southern Ontario."

Hamilton said, "Good idea—do you want me to follow up with the director? She and I came up through the ranks together."

Tom's boss replied. "Excellent idea, Bob. I didn't know you had a personal relationship. So that brings us back to what Al has found and how to proceed without letting Gerber know what we've found."

Hamilton took off his glasses and studiously cleaned them. "Well, there are a few alternatives: I can go to head office and ask them for a Ministerial Request to be made to the relevant Treasury Secretary in Washington for the New York office of the Internal Revenue Service to issue the equivalent of a Demand to the bank for information on the account in question as well as details of any other accounts the account holder has. That should take about three months, if we're lucky. Alternatively, you can bring in the Mendes woman, show her what you found and see if she talks. But that risks her telling Gerber, which she most probably will, and him taking off. Another alternative is for Tom to see what the trucks insured in Barrie are used for; and, maybe we can get a Demand for Porter Airlines to provide passenger information about the Mendes woman, and Gerber, to see how often they fly to New York."

"The last assumes they always fly. If they drive on occasion it will be hard to get border crossing information from the U.S. authorities," replied Tom's boss.

Tom had been listening carefully. He stated, "I agree we should follow up on the tractors insured by the company in Barrie. I also agree confronting Mendes is premature, it could spook them. Director, why don't you start the Ministerial Request process? I know it's a long shot. And could you authorize a Demand for Porter, and you might as well do one for Air Canada and WestJet as well. In addition, Al can give you the name of the bank the personal charge card was issued by and maybe we can issue a Demand there and get all her statements for the last year or two. That might tell us about travel to New York, and other places. That will cover those bases.

"And finally, when you follow up with the director of SI in London, just ask her to request the files for the courier company personally, if she can. We need to minimize the number of people in the loop. In the meantime, since Al says the audit of her tax returns didn't turn up anything untoward, maybe he can ask her to come in to go over his findings."

Turning to Al Edwards, he continued, "Maybe tell her you're having trouble reconciling her travel expenses and ask if she has anymore documentation. Give her a few days to pull it together." Again, turning to the director and looking at his boss, Tom opined, "So far, all we have is circumstantial evidence. I'm afraid that, in the end, we're going to have to raid the house and see what records we can find."

The director responded, "I like your reasoning, Tom. I'll get started on the Ministerial requests for the IRS to be expedited—we have a case of tax evasion and fraud that could prove massive—and yes, I'll get the Demands for the airlines, but they won't be overly cooperative from past experience. And I agree we will probably have to do a raid, but let's not go there yet. Thank you, gentlemen. And Al, you're to be commended for your diligence in the initial audit, which raised this issue. And Tom, keep at it. We've got a live one here with a lot of potential. But that is all we have at the moment, potential. I'll call Sheila at the London office now, after you leave."

The three gave their thanks and left the director to work on his part of the undertaking.

CHAPTER 11

On the following Monday, things started moving quickly at the local level. Tom received an email from Sandy McLean that had some interesting information. She had gone through various books on collectibles and antiques and reached the conclusion that the value of the items she had listed or photographed were worth in the neighbourhood of $750,000. And, later that same day, Tom had got a call on his personal cell phone from the real estate agent that had listed the house on Fig Tree way that a conditional offer had come in. So, time was precious.

Tom called Al and told him about the value of the collectibles and antiques. Al hadn't yet called Ms. Mendes about asking for further information. He had been busy with another file as he didn't want to rush contacting her. He wanted to delay in case other information had come to light, and both he and Tom were glad he had.

"Al, now that we have an estimate of what the value of the collectibles and antiques in the house are, ask her to come in again. You can couch it as you have a few questions about certain expenses. I'll follow up with my boss and you follow up with yours—I'd like to sit in on the interview and then spring the value of the furnishings on her. In no way does her income allow for that type of investment. Then we'll see how she reacts. Maybe we can rattle her."

Al responded, "Sounds good, I'll talk to my boss when I hang up. When do you want to see her?"

"How about Wednesday of next week? In the meantime, we've served a Demand on the TD Bank for copies of her personal credit card statements going back two years. I'll try to expedite it and maybe we'll have them by the time of the interview," responded Tom.

Tom then went to his boss's cubicle and brought him up to date on what was going on, and the conditional offer on the house.

"Should we bring the agent into the loop?" asked Tom. "I know it's against protocol, but we need to know if the house sells and where they are moving."

"Sorry, Tom, while I share your concern about them moving, we just can't bring in a civilian to monitor what's going on. They are her clients—or at least the Mendes woman is—and we can't risk her telling her about our interest. And we really have no reason to ask her to find out where they are going.

"Why don't you ask Owen in the tech sector to keep an eye on the listing and see if he can find out where they move to? She, at least, will need to update her address for her driver's licence, OHIP, and charge cards almost immediately. Also, why don't you ask the agent to let you know if the conditional offer falls through or closes because you might be interested in making an offer? You can always back out."

"OK, boss, will do."

Unfortunately, as the director had anticipated, the airlines filed an objection to the Demand for Information on the grounds that it was overreach by the CRA. There were no reasonable grounds for it to request the information and it was, therefore, a fishing expedition. While the Department of Justice could argue the case, that would take a substantial amount of time, and time that the local office didn't have. Tom would have to hope that the TD charge card statements would provide information that they could take back to one or more of the airlines asking for passenger details.

The next day, Wednesday, the director called Tom and his boss into his office. "Well gentlemen, guess what, the London source deductions section could find no record of the courier company in Tillsonburg collecting and remitting source deductions. Sheila, my friend, requested the last two years tax returns for the company. And guess what? No returns have been filed, either corporate or GST."

"I guess that's not surprising," responded Tom, "given what we know about the way Gerber operates. Could you ask them to check for corporate registrations and see who the initial shareholders are?"

"That assumes he bothered registering the company," sighed Tom's boss.

They were silent for several minutes as they thought about a viable reason for sending an auditor to the company without arousing suspicion. An auditor couldn't just show up out of the blue, there had to be a reason, and since there were no source deduction or corporate returns to audit, there really wasn't a reason. Unless, of course, it was brought to the audit branch's attention that the company wasn't filing tax returns.

Then suddenly, the director expostulated, "I've got it! Back when I was training, don't ask how long ago Tom," just as Tom's mouth opened, "I heard that back in the old days, before the Internet and on-line news and advertising, each tax office had a small group of auditors who would read the classifieds in the newspapers and then, if something was interesting, they'd check to see if a tax return was filed. They'd look for key words, like discretion, low-cost, professional services, etc. Then, if they found no tax return had been filed, they'd put out a lead to Audit to follow-up. A lot of folks who offered 'handyman' services were picked up that way."

"You're kidding!" exclaimed Tom.

"No, I remember hearing about that too," said his boss. "Led to some really interesting audits. Especially with companies or individuals who wanted to avoid leaving a trail."

"Where did we get folks to just read the classifieds?" asked a baffled Tom, who had come of age in the digital world.

"They were a collection of people; some were older auditors near retirement and wouldn't have time to complete a full audit before retirement, others had been hurt—not necessarily on the job—and coming back from sick leave, but not yet well enough to go out, and others just needed a break," replied the director.

He continued, "We've got the technical support group that does research for us now."

Tom interjected, "Yes, I used them to track down the original tax preparer for Mendes."

"Exactly," responded the director. "Why don't we ask Owen Charles and his team to come up with a rationale for paying the courier company a visit? Maybe they can find some advertising on the web and then we have a reason to 'visit' the operation."

"Great idea!" exclaimed Tom's boss. "Tom, you follow up with Charles and let him know it's urgent."

CHAPTER 12

Tom dropped by Owen's cubicle on his way back to the desk and told him what was needed and that it was most urgent. Owen said he'd get right on it.

Back at his desk, Tom reviewed where they were in the third-party review. It was clear that they couldn't keep the audit confidential for ever. He still hadn't followed up with Centrina, so he picked up the phone.

"Hello," answered a female voice.

"Hello, is the manager in please?" asked Tom.

"He is, but he's with a client right now. Could someone else help you?"

"I'd prefer to speak to the manager. I'm in Kitchener, but we're looking to buy an RV from a dealer near Barrie and my agent said that you folks specialize in RV and truck insurance. He suggested I might get a better price through you than my own insurer. Is that right?"

"Yes, we do specialize in large RVs—which are really trucks in disguise—as well as highway tractors, trailers, and other large vehicles. I didn't realize we were that well known."

"Well, you are. Anyway, my name is Tom Thomas—don't laugh—it wasn't my choice! Can you have the manager call me at this number, 519-555-8899 when he's free? Thank you," said Tom as he hung up.

Half an hour later he got a call from the manager at Centrina. "Mr. Thomas? Hello, my name his Hop Wilson, I'm the manager. I understand you're buying a large RV and are interested in getting an insurance quote. Correct?"

"I'm sorry for the subterfuge, I'm an investigator with the Canada Revenue Agency, but my name really is Tom Thomas."

"Mr. Thomas," replied the manager, more formally, "how do I really know you are with the CRA and not some scam artist?"

"Well, I'm not telling you that you owe money and need to pay by credit card or money order for one thing. My CRA identification number is 214568, and my full name is Thomas Thomas. If you want to confirm my identity, you can call our switchboard at 519-555-2121 and ask for me by name. Or if you prefer, we can arrange a time to meet and I can travel to your office," replied Tom.

"Thank you, Mr. Thomas. No, that won't be necessary, depending on what information you are after."

Tom continued, "Thank you, Mr. Wilson. I appreciate the cooperation. First, let me advise you that this request is confidential, and you are not to advise the client of my request. Is that clear?"

After a short pause, "Yes."

"Thank you. I'm looking for copies of insurance policies for six highway tractors that are owned by a company named Mambrino. According to vehicle registration records I've obtained you are the insurer of record. Do you need the VIN for each tractor?"

"No, I can look up the company and send you those details. What exactly do you need?" responded Wilson.

Tom listed off his requirements, including a copy of the application and the signatures of the applicant. He then asked Wilson to scan the documents and email them to him as well to mail him a photocopy, certified as true copies. He thanked Wilson for his assistance, reminded him of the confidential nature of his enquiry and then hung up.

Tom received a call from Al Edwards, "Tom, has anything come of the Demand to the TD Bank?"

"Not yet," replied Tom.

"Just wondering" replied Al. "I've got Jacqueline Mendes coming in on Wednesday, and I hoped we'd have more information before then."

"What time is she coming?" asked Tom.

"Ten," replied Al.

"Let's get together tomorrow morning for a couple of hours, along with both of our bosses, and come up with a plan. Maybe we can work with what we've got. Tell her we've requested information from the bank and the IRS about the New York bank and see if we can scare her into admitting what's going on."

"OK, I'll talk to my boss. We'll come up to your floor."

CHAPTER 13

The next morning, Tom called the real estate agent and asked if the conditional offer had been accepted. She told him it hadn't. But she understood that a clean offer was expected within the next twenty-four hours and she had gone back to the agent representing the couple who had made the conditional offer to see if they wanted to waive the conditions. Also, she had let them know that they would have to increase their offer, depending on what the new purchase offer was.

Tom thanked her and, letting on he and his wife might still be interested, asked to be notified of the outcome. Maybe they couldn't afford a house in that area if the price was too far above asking.

Promptly at 10:00 a.m. Al and his boss arrived, and Tom and his boss met them in the small conference room.

Al started by laying out what he had found in the Mendes audit. "Essentially this is a no change file. All her revenues and expenses are confirmed by invoices and receipts. All the invoice amounts were deposited into the business account and the claimed expenses match her business charge card, cheques written, and bills. But she does show a revenue amount from our phantom company—Mambrino. The total amount invoiced is $20,250, or about one-eighth of her revenue. So, if she knows Mambrino is not filing tax returns, why would she declare the income?"

Tom's boss interrupted, "Remind me what she does again?"

"She does financial consulting work. Sort of acts as a chief financial officer or advisor with respect to clients setting up budgets, preparing income statements, etc. She specializes in small companies that can't afford that sort of in-house expertise," responded Al.

"Does she prepare tax returns?"

"Not so far as I've been able to determine. Mostly budgeting, cost accounting, preparing income statements and balance sheets that are intended for lending institutions, but they could be used by a tax preparer as well," replied Al.

"Hmm," Tom's boss drummed his fingers on the table, "So if she is doing work for Mambrino, maybe it is legitimate—or gives the appearance of it. Maybe she is doing budgets and income statements for Gerber and doesn't know he isn't filing returns. Even if she does know, he still needs a budget to figure out expenses to make sure he is making a profit. But, given her background, is she naive enough to include the income from illegitimate business in her income?"

"Do we know that their relationship is?"

"No. She lists her status as single on her tax returns," replied Al.

"So, if she is naive, then why does she have a separate charge card that shows flights and hotel charges in New York City that coincide with the dates of deposits in the US bank account? Al, were there no names on that account?" asked Tom.

"No, it was the second page of a statement and so it had the bank's name and account number on it, the owners weren't listed. But I think it's a personal charge card as those expenses weren't claimed as business expenses," responded Al. "It seems she just comingled a personal charge statement, and not only the whole statement, with her business expenses.

"So, we don't know for certain that she has anything to do with the US bank or that she even went to NYC," stated Tom's boss. "She could have paid for tickets for Gerber to go to NYC and the account could be his. Just the paperwork got mixed up in her files."

"So, are you saying we shouldn't confront her with the charge card and US account information?" asked Tom.

"No, I'm not saying that. But I wish we had the TD Bank charge card statements; we need to be careful. After all, the trips could simply be a short vacation, although I'll give you that the timing does not seem coincidental, given the timing of the deposits to the US account. What was the exchange rate at that time? Anybody check?"

"Why is that important?" asked Al.

"Well, I was just thinking, you can't take more than $10,000 into or out of the US in cash. So maybe he had more Canadian currency, but after conversion it was the amount of the deposit?"

"Interesting thought," said Al and Tom simultaneously.

Al agreed to follow up on the conversion rates at the time of the deposits, although the conversion could have occurred here or in the U.S.

That brought them back to the questions of what to do next. Al reminded them that Jacqueline Mendes was scheduled to come in the following morning, Wednesday, for his final meeting with her.

Tom said, "Why don't I go to the meeting with Al. I can pretend to be his boss—no offence—and maybe I can raise the US bank account, just as a question. You know, just ask her if she was aware that she needed to declare foreign assets in excess of $100,000. An informal reminder. Since we don't have her name on the account, it will give her a chance to deflect the question as to name the real owner. Then follow up about the flights and deposits and see what sort of reaction we get. If need be, we can get into Mambrino and her relationship with Gerber. After all, we have her signature on the purchase agreement for the car she is driving, but is owned by Mambrino. Maybe even note that we know her house is listed and remind her to send a change of address."

Interesting, agreed both bosses. And while everyone in the room would have been happy to have the bank statements from TD, this appeared to be the best that could be done at this time.

Tom's boss raised the question as to whether to raise the income for Mambrino and ask her directly if she knew that it wasn't filing tax returns. They all agreed that they may have to do that, but that was to be a last resort question. Not that they were concerned about her reaction, but more about what Gerber's might be if she went home and confronted him, assuming she didn't know it was a phantom company. They were also hoping for information from the London office about the courier company in Tillsonburg.

They all agreed that was the best they could do for today, closed up their binders and headed back to their desks. Tom stopped Al and suggested they go to lunch, grab a beer, and run through their strategy for the next morning's meeting.

After lunch, Tom checked his email and found one from the manager at Centrina. It turned out that while the trucks were owned by Mambrino, as in the other two cases the insurance premiums were paid by the company they had been leased to. So, this tended to confirm that all that was paid to Mambrino was the net amount of the lease payment.

CHAPTER 14

WEDNESDAY

Both Tom and Al arrived at the office in good time to review their notes and their strategy again. Both were wearing suits, Tom in blue, Al in light tan, given it was late May and the weather was getting warmer. Al went down and let in Jacqueline Mendes, who was wearing taupe slacks and a white blouse, with conservative heels, and escorted her to the small meeting room. Tom was already there.

"Hello, Ms. Mendes," greeted Tom as he extended his hand.

She looked at him and then at Al, giving his hand a perfunctory shake.

Al said, "Tom is an associate of mine. I asked him to sit in on our meeting. Please take a seat."

Tom and Al sat on one side of the table, and Jacqueline on the other side. Al had some file folders in front of him, and Tom had a few in front of him as well. Her files she had left with Al some time ago were boxed neatly at the end of the table.

Al began, "Thank you for coming in, Ms. Mendes. I've gone through your tax returns for the past two years and the invoices, receipts, and bank statements you left with me, and I can tell you that

I found nothing amiss in your tax returns. So, in plain language, it is what we call a 'no change file' and that's good. It means you properly declared your income and expenses for the years in question. I can also tell you that that is very rare, probably only one in ten audits comes out like that."

Jacqueline relaxed a bit, "Whew, I'm relieved I can tell you. This is the first time I've ever been audited. In fact, it's the first time my tax returns have ever been questioned by the tax department. I've had friends who had some expenses disallowed—"

"What type?" interjected Al.

"Oh, some medical expenses that were claimed. They were asked just to mail their medical expenses to the PEI office and then they got a letter back saying that such and such an expense was not allowable under the Income Tax Act. But no one I know has ever been called into the local office and actually had their invoices and expenses gone through by an auditor."

Al responded, "That's probably because they were just claiming medical expenses and maybe it was the first time they did, so the PEI office just wanted to make sure the expenses being claimed were allowable. There is a list in the Act, section 118.2 that specifically lists the types of medical expenses that are allowable. Even then, the medical expenses have to exceed a certain threshold. No, the reason you were audited is that you have a business and your business hadn't been audited before. We try to audit independent business every few years just to make sure no unintended errors have been made, like maybe mixing up numbers on an expense or when entering income from an invoice. Of course, if the audit shows that income wasn't included, as an example, then that business maybe audited again the next year or the year after, just to make sure there isn't a pattern of not reporting income."

Tom then asked, "Out of curiosity, since this is the first time you've been audited, how long have you been in business as a financial consultant?"

Jacqueline responded, "I've been self-employed for the past three years. I used to work in the finance area of a large company but got downsized four years ago. The severance I got specifically forbade me from getting another job for a period of time, so I was just sitting around the house, and I was getting bored. Then my boyfriend suggested I set up my own consulting business. My former employer didn't need to know right away, and I could take a year to get it up and running—find clients and so on. And before the end of the first year my severance payments would be exhausted. In fact, my boyfriend has a company and he agreed to be my first client! He is an amazing man!"

"By the way, your tax return indicates you are single. Did you know you could claim married or equivalent to married, i.e., common-law, and may be eligible for some additional benefits, such as splitting investment income, assuming it is in both your names?" stated Al.

"Yes, I was aware of that. But since his business has much more income than mine, we decided that really wasn't of benefit right now, so we're both filing as single."

Tom asked congenially, "When did you two meet?"

"About the time I was let go. I was drowning my sorrows in a neighbourhood pub and he struck up a conversation. We liked each other and started dating and moved in together about six months later. Why?"

"Well, in all honesty Ms. Mendes, Al came to me with a question—I've been around longer than him and he was wondering that even though you make a good income from your business, how you could afford the house you own on Fig Tree Way? It just seemed a little out of line with your income. Did you receive an inheritance of some sort?"

She laughed, "No, nothing like that. My boyfriend owned a small house that was fully paid for, and I still had a mortgage on my condo. He suggested, when we decided to move in together, that we both sell our properties and buy a nice house. He had more money than me, but he insisted the house be in my name only. I don't know why for certain. Maybe he thought if we did break up, I'd have the house as compensation or something."

Al enquired, tentatively, "Your boyfriend sounds like quite a guy. What's he do for a living?"

"He owns a trucking company. He leases trucks to companies; they pay the expenses and just pay him the net lease amount. That reduces his paperwork a lot and means he doesn't have to hire staff. And he recently set up a small courier business somewhere in southwest Ontario. I don't know exactly where. Why?"

"Would this company's name be Mambrino? And would your boyfriend by any chance be Harold Gerber?" queried Tom, his tone becoming more official.

"Yes. That's right. Why? Is Harry in trouble?"

"You could say that," responded Tom. "Al, please bring Ms. Mendes up to date."

Jaqueline Mendes looked at Tom, and then at Al, her face changing into a semi-shocked look.

Al started, "Some four years ago your boyfriend was taken to court by the CRA for failing to file tax returns. He subsequently was fined and filed four years' worth of meaningless tax returns. I know. I spent a hundred hours trying to verify the income and expenses he claimed and couldn't. I even found a purchase agreement for a car in your driveway—a BMW—and he denied it was his signature. After a hundred hours, I had to wrap up the file, but referred it to Special Investigations."

Mendes, a shocked look on her face said, "Special Investigations?"

"That's me," said Tom matter-of-factly. "Special Investigations is a unit of the CRA that investigates fraud, maleficence, and tax evasion. Since Al referred this file to us some six months ago, we have been looking into your boyfriend's business affairs. Would it surprise you to know that his company, Mambrino, hasn't ever filed a tax return? And since he was taken to court and forced to file four years of returns, he hasn't filed a personal one since. He is a very bad boy and, actually, we hope you can answer some questions for us."

"What? *No!* That's not right. I do financial statements for him!"

"We know. And we know you are an honest person, Jaqueline," sympathized Al as he reached his hand across the desk towards her, "We know, because you declared the consulting income for his business, but there are things we hope you will help us with."

Tom went on, "To be honest, you weren't a target in our investigation into Mr. Gerber, but we knew you owned the house he lived in, and we hoped that by auditing you we might get some insight into his business, and we have. In fact, our third-party investigation has told us a lot, but not everything."

"Third party?" questioned a confused Jacqueline Mendes.

"Sorry. A third-party audit is when we can't determine an individual's or company's income and expenses through a normal audit, such as the one Al did on you. Here we're talking about someone undertaking perhaps, a form of criminal activity or wilfully setting out to evade the proper payment of tax on their income. And that's what we've been doing the past three months. We found how many trucks, vans, and cars your boyfriend owns. We know the companies that insure them. And we know the companies they are leased to. We're in the process of getting from those companies the amounts they have paid to Mambrino over the past several years. We even know that one of the cars was bought by you, Ms. Mendes, so you'll forgive me if I don't share Mr. Edwards' view of your honesty. And we found a couple of things in your files that didn't quite belong, to be honest."

"What things? What are you talking about? Harry is a good man, a loving man! Damn it!" cried a distraught Jacqueline Mendes.

Tom opened the file folder in front of him. He pulled out the partial charge card statement, showing the payment for the flight to New York City and hotel and then the bank statement from the bank in New York City. "What do you know about these two statements?"

She looked at them. "The charge card statement charge is for a trip to New York Tom took. Just overnight. He said he had a business meeting. I have no idea about the bank account. I never knew about it."

Tom queried, "Then why would it be amongst your records?"

"I have no idea," responded Jacqueline. Sometimes our files do get mixed up and maybe it got put into my file for last year by accident. But the statement doesn't even have a name or address on it? How do you know it's Harry's?"

"Well, you have a point. Except that the dates of one deposit coincide with the date of the trip and hotel stay. So, yes, admittedly it's circumstantial. But we are so confident that this means something that a Ministerial Request has been approved. That means that a request has gone to the Internal Revenue Agency's head office in Washington to have agents in the New York office obtain the bank records for this account, as well as any other information the bank has about the person who owns the account."

"Just what do you suspect?" asked Mendes, now more composed and professional.

"Well, we haven't been able to find any bank account associated with Mambrino. We'd like to know who owns that charge card. But to answer your question: everything points to Mr. Gerber conducting systematic tax evasion, which is an offence that can result in a significant fine and prison time. The company has a very small footprint. It doesn't file tax returns. It has client companies that pay most, if not all, of the operating expenses for the trucks, and only net amounts are paid to the company. No payroll deductions, no tax returns. Where's the money go? It appears that at least some ends up in a New York bank. The courier company in Tillsonburg is being raided, as we speak, by the Special Investigations unit in London. It hasn't filed returns either and maybe we'll get a lead as to where the profits go from there."

"This is overwhelming," sighed Jacqueline Mendes. "And yes, I signed for one of the cars for Harry's company. He was on another one of his trips to New York and the car dealership called and said it was ready. He'd already given them permission to let me sign the sales agreement if he was out of town. But that's all. And yes, I guess it looks bad, but he told me I could use it. I asked him about personally using a car owned by his company. He told me not to worry, he'd make sure it was treated as a taxable benefit to himself."

"I'm sorry," Al interjected, "but did he use those exact words?"

"Yes, Harry is very knowledgeable about tax and stuff. That's one of the reasons we hit it off so well. He has a master's degree in economics. In fact, he lectured in tax at one of the universities. This comes as a real surprise to me. I just don't know what to say. What to do? This is all so confusing."

Both Al and Tom sat in shocked silence for several seconds. The revelation that Gerber was an economist and had taught income tax at the university level was a bombshell. No wonder he was so good at hiding money. Why hadn't this come up earlier? The simple answer was no one had thought to look into his background. Not that you would. It was a simple case of failure to file returns, no history to look at because you didn't need to look for one. Simple case, a guy—maybe like others who think income tax is not legal—decides to conduct business in a way that doesn't give rise to a money trail, or at least one easily followed. Not Al's fault. He did all that was expected of him, given the known facts.

Tom recovered first, "How long ago did Mr. Gerber teach? Did he tell you?"

Mendes thought for a moment, "He really didn't say. But if I recall it was right after school, after he got his master's. I think he taught for maybe five years."

Tom said quietly, "Ms. Mendes, we are truly sorry for springing this on you, but we needed to know if, or how, you were involved in Mr. Gerber's business. Tell me, have you ever accompanied Mr.

Gerber to New York or to other places outside of Canada? If so, were you aware he kept money outside of the country?"

She replied, "I've gone to New York with Harry several time. Sometimes we'd go to see a show, sometimes he had business meetings. And we've been to other places and been on cruises, but when we did those, he didn't have business meetings."

"Where did the money come from for these trips?"

"Mostly Harry paid, although when it came to cruises, I'd pay part of the cost."

"Is that charge account we showed you yours?"

"No."

"Do you have a personal charge card and bank account?"

"Yes."

"We need copies of your personal charge account and bank statements, both savings and chequing, for the past two years as well as any investment statements you held, either jointly with Mr. Gerber or personally. And also, do you know where Mr. Gerber banks?"

A shaken Jacqueline Mendes replied, "I can get you my charge account and bank statements fairly quickly. I organize everything by year. And I keep a record of my investments in a file as well as online. As to Harry's business, I'm not involved in that other than preparing financial statements for him."

"Do you have access to those financial statements?"

"I can probably find them, I keep copies on my computer or back-up files, as I do for all clients. If you give me your email address, I can send you those when I get home."

"Out of curiosity, how profitable is Mr. Gerber's company?"

"He's doing quite well, if I remember that last income statement correctly. His net profit was about $75,000."

"Ms. Mendes, I need to caution you that, while you appear to be an honest person, your boyfriend isn't. You are not to tell him anything about what was discussed today beyond that you were found not to owe any income tax and that your records were in order. Any mention of our investigation into Mr. Gerber could be construed as you being an accessory in his tax evasion scheme. And that is what it looks like. In fact, because of his tax knowledge, it could be a criminal investigation. Do you understand?" stated Tom as formally as he could.

"Yes, I understand," stated Mendes. "But how long is this going to take? I mean I have to live with him, act normal, even though I'm now aware I may be living with a criminal? I don't know how long I can do that," she said as a tear rolled down a cheek.

Al looked at Tom and then whispered in his ear. Tom nodded.

"Ms. Mendes, when is the next time Mr. Gerber is planning on going to New York without you? asked Tom.

"Ahhh, I think next week sometime, but the date isn't set yet."

"Ms. Mendes, I know this a lot to ask. When you know he is going, please call Al. You have his number? We were thinking we would need to get a search warrant to enter your house and search for records of Mr. Gerber's company. But you own the house, so we're asking your permission to enter your house and search it. We'll get the wording sorted out with our legal people to make sure you are protected legally. And if you can gather any information about Mr. Gerber's business in the meantime, without leading to questions, we would really appreciate it. Is that all right or would you prefer we get a warrant?" stated Tom.

"No, you don't need a warrant. I'll cooperate," answered a dejected Jacqueline Mendes. "Is that all? May I go now?"

"Yes," answered Tom, "that's all. And thank you for your cooperation. I'm sure this has come as a shock."

"You don't know the half of it. It's a lot to absorb and then go home and pretend everything is all right."

Al said, "Those files are heavy, I'll help you carry them down to your car. OK?"

"Yes, thank you. That would be kind of you," sighed Jacqueline.

On the way down the elevator Al asked, as if incidentally, "Oh, Ms. Mendes, my wife and I were out for a drive a week or so ago and noticed there was a for sale sign on your lawn. Where are moving to?"

A now wary Jacqueline asked, "Why were you driving by my house?"

"Oh, we have kids and we're thinking about moving to a bigger house so we often go on drives through neighbourhoods looking at houses."

"Isn't the Mulberry area a little out of your price range? I'm not being nosey, but I wouldn't think you'd be able to afford it."

"Well, my wife's uncle died six months ago and he didn't have any family, so he's leaving everything to his nieces and nephews and the lawyer has told my wife she is a beneficiary and will probably receive a decent amount, something in the mid-six figures, once the estate costs have been paid," improvised Al.

"Oh, well, we've bought a house in New Hamburg and Harry's business is doing well enough we're thinking about buying two or three condominiums in that new building they are talking about building in downtown Kitchener as investments. As the new house isn't that expensive, we'll use some of the proceeds from the sale of our—my—house plus some of Harry's money. We'll own our house free and clear and then put mortgages on the rentals to offset some of the income for a while. We don't want to work forever and so we thought between rental income and capital appreciation the condos would be good long-term investments. But I guess that's out the window now," sighed Jacqueline.

"OK, I know this upsetting. But please, I need that address in New Hamburg in case you move before we finish this case."

"It's 2323 Nithview Drive. I don't know the postal code offhand."

"Thank you, that's all I need for now. Take care of yourself. Let us know when he is going, and I'm sure this will be over for you soon. I know it's hard to find someone you love is, perhaps, a criminal. But there is a chance, a slim chance, that there is more to this than we know, and it can be explained. Maybe go for a drive or visit a friend and calm down before going home. You're sure you'll be OK?"

"Yes, I'll be fine. I'm a big girl, and I can figure this out. It's just a surprise, a shock really. But I'll get over it. I'll call you when I know what time he's leaving."

She opened the trunk of her car and Al put the file boxes into it and watched, silently, as she got into her car and drove out of the parking lot and turned right onto Frederick Street. He sighed and headed back into the office.

CHAPTER 15

When Al got back to the meeting, he found both bosses there and Tom had loosened his tie. He shook his head and did the same thing.

After they had brought their bosses up to date on recent developments, and the ground breaking discovery that Gerber had lectured on income tax. All four sat at the conference table and thought.

"You said, Tom, that she gave us verbal permission to enter her house when Gerber is away," confirmed Tom's boss. Both Tom and Al nodded. "I know the house is in her name, but you also told us," looking at Al's boss, "that Gerber helped pay for it. So, while she is the legal owner, her boyfriend helped pay for it. I think I'd be more comfortable if we got Legal involved and got a warrant. That way she's protected, she didn't let us in on her own accord, so she has some legal protection in that we had a search warrant. And we have protection because of the search warrant. I'll talk to the director about getting one expedited when we leave here. I'll also follow up with the local detachment of the Queen's Cowboys and get a couple of fellows from both white collar and criminal divisions come and join in the fun. Might want some local support as well, I'll see what the boss says. But many hands make labour light, as the old saying goes."

Tom spoke, "I don't think we need local support. She'll cooperate. I'm sure she will look for those charge card and New York bank statements that she wasn't aware of. And she'll have her own charge card, bank, and investment material for us. In fact, she said she'd email what she had online to Al."

"You sound pretty sure she didn't know what was going on, Tom. Al, do you agree?"

"Yes, she was pretty shaken up when Tom hit her with the US information and charge statement. I think, at minimum, she'll have a pretty good idea about where his business materials are in the house."

They all sat there again for a few minutes. "Good job guys, this was a tremendous breakthrough. Al, you want to join us for the raid?" said Tom's boss.

Al looked at his boss, "I'd really like that, if it's OK?"

Al's boss said, "Go! You earned it!"

CHAPTER 16

Nothing much happened on the file until two days later. On the Friday, the results of the Demand on the TD Bank came through and three years of charge card statements were delivered to the Frederick Street office. The charge card was a corporate card in the name of Mambrino and the address listed was a suite number on Fairway Avenue. A quick check of Google revealed that the 'suite number' was actually a UPS store on Fairway. Tom wondered what else got delivered there and went to talk to his boss.

They agreed that was interesting. It wasn't too far from where Gerber lived and so was a convenient mail drop. It also gave some semblance of credibility to the company to have an address with 'suite' in it. Do they need a warrant or Demand or could they just go see the owner? Off to see the director again to get his reaction, as well as bring him up to speed.

The director felt that the UPS store was a secondary target. Maybe the raid would show what other mail got delivered there. After all, the cheques from the client companies had to get to Gerber somehow. On that thought, the director picked up the phone and called his opposite number in London.

"Sheila, Bob here. Just wondered how the auditors and payroll people made out at the courier company." He listened.

"Really? That's great! Did they come across an address where they mailed the net revenue cheques to? That's great, thanks, Sheila. Let me know what else your people find." He hung up and said to Tom and his boss, "OK, the cheques for the net amount of revenue are mailed bi-weekly to the same address on Fairway. The auditors discovered that the employees claim to be self-employed contractors. Their T-1s are being checked to confirm that. There is also a local business account that the local manager uses to pay expenses and where client cheques are deposited so only the net amount is sent to Gerber. Seems like a pattern, doesn't it? Sheila will let me know the results of the audit. Tom, why don't you follow up with the other clients we know about and just confirm where they are sending their lease cheques. I suspect it is the same place. Now we need to know what he's doing with the money.

"Good work so far. Now we know where the money is going, and from where, we can do a net worth audit, at least sort of. If we go back two years and get each company to send us what they paid Mambrino each month, and check for expenses, like the insurance, maybe we can get a picture of revenue and expenses."

Tom interrupted the director's chain of thought, "Sorry, but I found from the insurance companies that the client companies were paying the insurance directly."

"You're right, Tom. That had slipped my mind. But still we can get an estimate of net revenue."

After Tom and his boss left the director's office, Tom's boss said, "That's a good idea. Follow up with the two companies that lease the trucks and ask the finance managers to send us copies of the cheques and invoices for the past two—no, make it back to the original contract dates with Mambrino. Tell them we know it's a lot of work and also not to disclose any information to any Mambrino representative. This is now a case of tax evasion and will probably result in criminal prosecution. You can also tell them that, to our knowledge, they had nothing to do with whatever we are investigating. There is no need to be concerned with any potential liability on their company's part."

Tom gave his boss a 'will do' and headed back to his cubicle. Once there, he picked up the phone.

"Owen, Tom here." After the pleasantries Tom continued "Owen, remember you checked on a Harold Gerber for me? We know he doesn't have a social media presence and you couldn't find any banking or financial information for him personally, but it has recently come to our attention that his company, Mambrino, has a corporate credit card with TD Bank. And we also now have a corporate address, it's a mailbox at the UPS store on Fairway. Just wondering if I give you that information if you could do some more research based on the company, name, location and what banking info we have?"

"Sure, no problem. That should make it easy."

"That's great, and oh, by the way, we also know that he, his company, or Jacqueline Mendes, has a US bank account. We don't have a number, but we've sent a request to the IRS to get that information for us. But I wondered if you could shortcut that search?"

"I'll try but getting stuff from a US bank could be construed as hacking..." replied Owen.

"Try to stay within the law. The name of the bank is Third Manhattan Bank of New York, here's the location."

"Will see what I can come up with."

"Thanks, Owen, keep me in the loop."

CHAPTER 17

Nothing happened on the Monday related to the case: no reply from Owen Charles; no word from Jacqueline Mendes as to when Gerber was going to New York that week; and nothing from the companies that were leasing the trucks from Mambrino. Tom knew it would take a while for them to get the requested information together, make copies and mail them to him. He assumed that's how the info would arrive as he had requested a lot and it might be too big a package to send as an attachment. Time passes slowly when you're waiting. Tom re-read the file.

Tuesday came and the morning passed slowly. More waiting. He did get an email from one of the companies that leased trucks letting him know they were mailing him copies of invoices for the past two years. They would send the rest of the requested information later as it was in off-site storage. They were in the process of transferring the old files to their computer systems, but scanning was taking some time, and they weren't sure if the old invoices had been scanned yet.

Even though he didn't have all the information yet, he killed some time by setting up an Excel spreadsheet so he could enter the monthly income amounts from each client company and total the yearly income from each source and get an annual total.

That afternoon, Owen sent Tom an email. From what he found out: the corporate charge card was all Mambrino had with TD bank. He hadn't found a corporate chequing account so he asked Tom to check the TD statements and see if they noted how the invoices amounts were paid. Tom hadn't paid much attention to the corporate charge cards statements up to that point, other than a cursory glance, which told him not much was charged, other than flights to and from, and hotels in New York City.

Tom checked a couple of charge statements and found that they were noted as paid by cash. Interesting. Where did the cash come from? He sent a reply to Owen and waited. Just before 4:00 p.m., Al called him and told him that the Mendes woman had called him: Gerber was going to New York Thursday, coming back late in the day. Tom called his boss and the wheels were set in motion.

While his boss let the director know, Tom called the inspector in charge of the Kitchener RCMP office. As the director had previously given the inspector a heads up, Tom's call was anticipated. Inspector Smith said that he would have two constables from the white-collar crime division and a sergeant from the criminal investigation branch meet Tom and others from the CRA at the Tim Hortons on Fairway Road at eight on Thursday morning. From there they would make their way to Gerber's house on Fig Tree Way, which was about a ten-minute drive.

After he hung up, Tom sent an email with the details to Al, the director and both bosses. He suggested that five of them meet the next morning to make sure everyone knew their roles.

CHAPTER 18

Thursday morning arrived. Tom put on a sports jacket he kept for just such occasions. It was a tweed jacket with leather elbow patches and a leather patch on the right front shoulder, where the stock of a rifle or shotgun might rest. This was a jacket he had had since joining the Special Investigations unit a decade ago. In all that time, he had only worn it maybe a half-dozen times, when he actually went on a raid to seize a taxpayer's records.

Lisa looked at her husband and said, "Be careful, Tom." She was always concerned when he went on a raid and give him a big hug and a kiss on the lips.

"I will. He is supposed to be out of town and the woman he lives with is cooperating with us, so it shouldn't be an issue. See you tonight."

He left and drove to the Tim Hortons rendezvous. It had been decided that only Tom's boss would accompany Tom and Al on the raid, so with the three members from the RCMP that made six in total. They decided to go in three cars and leave Al and Tom's bosses at the Tim Hortons. They could pick them up afterwards.

They left the Tim's at eight fifteen and were at 52 Fig Tree Way at eight twenty-five. Tom led the way to the front door, rang the doorbell and when Jacqueline Mendes answered, he presented her with the search warrant and introduced the other members of the team. Mendes already knew Al and was a little surprised to see him there.

She had started to collect Gerber's files, but there were more than she had anticipated. Some were in his 'office' and others were filed in boxes in the basement. But they couldn't just be satisfied that these were the only files. Al apologized and said they had to search the house. *Hasn't this guy heard of online storage?* wondered Tom.

After two hours of searching and collecting boxes and yes, some CDs, Tom said, "This isn't going to fit in the cars. We need a cube van."

One of the constables said, "We've got a van back at the office. I'll call and have it brought over."

Tom thanked him. "Ms. Mendes, we really appreciate your co-operation. Also, do you know if he had a personal bank account, or do you have a joint one?"

"So far as I'm aware he doesn't have a bank account. We don't have a joint account; he just gives me money monthly that I put in my account to pay the monthly expenses."

Al interjected, "What about the money he paid you for your financial services? Did he give you a cheque or cash?"

She had to think for a couple of minutes, "No, that was a lot of money. He gave me a money order."

"Didn't that seem strange to you? A money order instead of a corporate cheque?"

"I guess it would have, if it had been another client. But Harold was also tight with his business interests. He told me it was mostly a cash business so I guess in hindsight it should have raised a flag. But we're in love, we live together. I guess it never crossed my mind."

"If it's mostly cash and he doesn't have a bank account, where does he keep his money? Under the mattress, in a safe?"

That question was met with silence as Jacqueline Mendes just stared at the floor.

Just then, one of the constables came into the room. "Gentlemen, would you come with me, please?" Tom and Al and Tom's boss started to move toward the doorway, and Jacqueline started to follow. "Ma'am, please go into the front room and sit down, please," ordered the constable.

The three CRA men followed the constable while Jacqueline Mendes, looking confused, went into the sitting room at the front of the house and sat down. She looked at the door with a concerned expression on her face and held her hands and knees together tightly.

The constable led them into the dining room, which was nicely paneled with maple wainscoting. The sergeant said, "Gentlemen, look at this." He stepped aside, showing that one panel of the wainscoting was open, and inside was a small safe. It was a biometric wall safe, accessible using a fingerprint identification system. The safe used a biometric device feature, an optical scanner that analyzes the scanned fingerprint and compares it to unique characteristics of those stored in the device. In addition to the fingerprint recognition technology, this safe was secured by two motorized steel deadbolt locks. That type of safe should, according to the sergeant, have a backup opening system, which from the look of the safe meant a two-key system, like a safe deposit box.

"Wow," exclaimed Al. This was like something out of a spy thriller. Tom and his boss just looked.

The sergeant said, "I assume the biometrics—the fingerprint—is Gerber's. I wonder if the woman knows where the keys are. And, since this safe can store several fingerprints, I'd like to see she if she can open this."

Al said, "I'll get her."

He returned a few minutes later.

"Ms. Mendes," queried the sergeant in a stern voice, "have you seen this before?"

"No!"

"Even so, I'd like you to take your right thumb, then your left, and try to open it."

She did, silently. Then the sergeant requested she try the rest of her fingers. Nothing happened.

"This safe can be opened using two keys. Do you know where they are?"

"No! I've never seen this before."

"Tell me, Ms. Mendes, how would Mr. Gerber have had this safe installed without your knowledge? This is your house, right?"

"About six months ago he said he thought wainscoting would really dress up the dining room. He said he'd pay to have it done and to repaint the walls to complement it. Since he was willing to pay for it, I told him to go ahead. He hired a contractor and we stayed out of the room while the work was done. I guess he had this installed without telling me. I really don't know. This is all very confusing, very confusing," she replied, shaking her head and starting to cry. Al put his arm around her shoulders and led her back to the front room. He asked if she'd like a tea or coffee. She said a tea please, and he headed to the kitchen to make her one.

Back in the dining room, the sergeant said, "OK, gentlemen. This is an unexpected development. We need to look for those keys. Check everywhere, check every room. We are looking for two keys. The safe is made by Barska and there should be two brass keys with that name on the tab end. This is a fairly uncommon household safe. I'm going to call the office and ask for a couple more officers to come down and help us with the search. If we can't find it, we'll have to wait for Gerber to get home."

Tom asked, "If it's biometric, why does it also have keys?"

The sergeant replied, "Good question. The keys are a backup if there is only one person that has access. What happens if he or she ends up in hospital or dead? There needs to be a backup so that someone else can access the safe."

"So that is why you asked Ms. Mendes to try to open it, or if she knew where the keys are. If Gerber got hurt, you'd assume she would have access."

"Right. And that is why I'm surprised she doesn't. Does Gerber have any associates he might be in business with?"

Both Al and Tom shook their heads. They hadn't discovered a partner.

The sergeant continued, "I supposed if something happened to Gerber, the Mendes woman could have the safe drilled."

Al responded, "But she didn't seem to know about it."

"You're right," replied the sergeant, "or maybe she is just a good actress. If she really doesn't know, and he died and the house was sold, some new owner might find it in a day, a year or maybe never. And if they did, they might find a surprise, or nothing. Sort of like Geraldo Rivera's search for Al Capone's vault back in '86."

The sergeant started looking in the attic, working his way down; the constables from white collar crime started in the basement, coming next to the main floor while the sergeant moved from the attic to the second floor. Methodically, every drawer was opened, mattresses were moved and clothes pockets gone through. Tom, his boss and Al searched as well, although they didn't have the training. Noon came. Tom's boss said, "Al, you get the short straw. Check what people want for lunch. Keep it simple, no running to different places. I'll approve the expense if your boss won't." Al took a pad from his pocket and made the rounds.

By three they had been there for six and a half hours. The RCMP van had arrived and they loaded it with boxes of files and CDs. Anything that might prove useful. But they still hadn't found anything that looked like a matched pair of keys.

One of the new arrivals, a constable only three years out of Depot volunteered to get a garbage bag to clean up the leftovers from lunch. Jacqueline told him they were in the garage. He opened the door from the house and turned on the light. The garage was immaculate—the flooring and walls were done with sheathing that allowed tools to be hung neatly. There was a snow blower and lawn mower, as well as the usual assortment of spades and gardening tools hanging on the far wall. At the back of the garage there were three grey plastic storage cabinets, two large and a small one wall-mounted. He started to look in each for the garbage bags. He found them in the small cabinet, along with spare paper products. He decided that since he was in the garage, he'd look in the other two. The shelves in the first had more gardening materials, pots, fertilizer, small hand tools, along with ice melt and windshield washer fluid. The second had stuff for a car, like car wash and polish, dashboard cleaner and a power washer. But then he saw something that didn't quite belong. It was a small rectangular box, like a match box. He recognized it as a key box, the type that might fit under one of those garden ornaments that no one was supposed to know hid a key. He took a tissue out of his pocket and gently picked it up. Inside were two small brass keys with the name 'Barska' on the logo spot at the top of the key. He gently replaced it and went back to the house entrance. "Sarg, can you come into the garage please?"

The sergeant came to the door "What's up?"

"Come look at this," answered the constable as he led him over to the cabinet. "See that little box on the top shelf? I looked inside and there are two brass keys marked with the logo Barska on them. I didn't touch the keys. I put the box back in case you wanted a photo before we officially open it."

"Good thinking, lad." Turning to the door he called out: "Bring the camera!"

After the find was documented and taken out gently to be put into an evidence bag, the two keys were carefully removed and taken into the dining room. They were inserted into the key slots and turn simultaneously. The safe opened.

They all looked at the contents quietly for a few moments. Then the sergeant, being the senior officer, asked for pictures to be taken of the open safe, and then each item individually, *in situ*. After that, each item was removed and checked. The constables handled these duties while those from the CRA looked on and took notes.

"Sarg, I've got $75,000 cash in total here. Mostly twenties and fifties with some hundreds," said one of the constables. The other said, "And I've got $15,500 US in money orders."

"Where are the money orders from?" queried Al.

"Western Union," replied the constable.

That still left two items in the safe, a small rectangular box and a small black drawstring bag. Both were removed and photographed, then the box was opened. Inside was a US passport in the name of Warren White. The picture and birthdate matched Gerber's. Without saying anything, the black drawstring bag was opened and inverted over the table. Out tumbled a myriad of diamonds and sapphires. They all just looked at each other and Jacqueline, who was standing at the back, covered her mouth and then screamed, "*Oh my God, what's happening?*" bursting into tears and leaving the room.

"OK, everyone, let's pack up. Bag and tag boys, close up the safe and the wall panel." Everyone sprang into action. The young constable went about picking up fast food wraps and tidying the counters, even putting some dishes into the dishwasher.

After they had cleaned up, Al and Tom thanked Jacqueline for her cooperation. She had a copy of the search warrant and they told her, reinforced by the sergeant, that she was to be honest with her boyfriend. Yes, the house had been raided by the CRA and RCMP; they took a bunch of his files and CDs and had found a safe in the dining room wall. Since she was unaware of it she could get mad at him, tell him about the phoney passport and ask him what was going on. As they were leaving the sergeant put his hand on her shoulder, "Ms. Mendes, we are grateful for your co-operation, but Mr. Gerber will undoubtedly be upset. This was quite the shock for you. And he is definitely doing something illegal, whether it is tax avoidance or something more, we'll need to determine. Here's my card, if you ever need help or need to talk, please call me. What time is he due back?"

"About seven-thirty tonight, depending on traffic from Toronto."

"I'll have an unmarked car with two constables in it parked up the block starting at six tonight. I'll also arrange relief for them. So, if there any problems, run out the front door and they'll respond. We don't want you to get hurt."

"Thank you very much. This is very upsetting. To realize that the man you love isn't the person you thought he was. I'm still trying to process what you found today."

Tom's boss rode with the sergeant and Al with Tom back to the Tim Hortons where they had left their cars some eight hours earlier. Surprise! Al's boss's car was gone and a tow truck was in the process of hooking up Tom's boss's. The sergeant immediately went and spoke with the driver of the tow truck.

"What's happening?" he asked, as he identified himself.

"The manager complained about this car and another one taking up parking spaces all day so he called my company to come and get them. I'm just doing my job."

"OK, leave this car here. Where is the other one?"

He came over to Tom's car. "I'm sorry, the manager apparently complained about the cars being left here and called to have them towed." He handed Tom a card and said to Al, "Here's where your car is. You'll have to pay to get it back. But get them to call me before you pay, just in case. Hope you can expense it."

Tom's boss said, "It's been a long day. I'm going home. The two of you do the same after you get Al's car. We'll brief the director tomorrow."

Tom and Al shook their heads and Tom drove him to the yard. As the sergeant expected, Al was charged for the tow and storage. But, after the manager spoke with the sergeant, he agreed to only charge Al for the tow and not for storage. Al figured he'd be able to expense the fifty bucks it cost. *Oh well,* he thought, *even if I can't, it was worth the cost for what I learned today.*

As the CRA didn't have a secure area to store the cash and precious stones, the RCMP had taken them to their detachment where they made sure they were properly inventoried and witnessed and securely locked away.

CHAPTER 19

Tom got home latter than usual. Lisa said hi as he headed to the fridge and popped the top off a beer. He came into the living room. "What a day," he sighed, as he sat down on the chesterfield.

"What happened with the raid?" asked Lisa as she moved behind him and started to rub his shoulders. "Take off your jacket and I'll give you a bit of a massage." Tom shrugged off his jacket and set it aside as she continued a slow neck and shoulder massage.

"Well, the raid went off OK, but we found something we didn't anticipate."

"What?"

"A wall safe hidden behind wainscoting in the dining room. We finally found a set of keys and opened it. Ummm that feels good... anyway, there was lots of cash and a passport in another name." He took a pull on his beer as his wife moved around and knelt down before removing his shoes.

"So, this case is getting more and more interesting, eh?"

"Yes, it is, and I don't see closure anytime soon," replied Tom as his wife massaged his feet. "The RCMP left a cruiser to watch the house in case he hurts his wife."

"Why would he do that?"

"Don't think he would. She has a copy of the search warrant. But he might try to run too, and we don't want that."

"Do you have enough to arrest him?" she asked as she moved up, massaging his calves and thighs as she went.

"No, but maybe they could hold him so we can question him," replied Tom and took another pull on his beer, leaned back and ran the fingers of his left hand through her auburn hair.

As the massage ended, Tom said, "That felt great, sweetheart, I'll repay you this weekend."

"Come on, supper's ready," smiled Lisa as she headed towards the kitchen, swaying her hips.

CHAPTER 20

Tom was at the office bright and early on Friday. He met Al, his boss and Al's boss in his boss's office. They reviewed the previous day and just as Tom's boss was about to pick up the phone to call the director's secretary, his phone rang. It was the director's secretary requesting their presence at the director's office.

When they got there, Bob said, "I just got off the phone with Inspector Smith. He brought me up to date—"

Tom interjected, "We were just about to do that."

Hamilton waved him off, "So we have a real live one. False passport. Cash in a wall safe and jewels. The RCMP will take care of getting them appraised. What are your plans with Gerber?"

Tom started, "Well, I'm still waiting on invoices from one of the clients and the results of the audit in London, but I think we need to confront him now. He still has a passport, which I assume is in his name, but I won't know until I see it. Can we get that surrendered while I conduct the audit?"

"Not sure," replied the director. "I'll check with Legal. Maybe we can get the Mounties to move on that."

Tom continued, "I'll get hold of Owen Charles, give him the alternate name we found—Warren White—and details of both passports and see what he can find. But I agree, Bob, we need to get him in here for a meeting. Do you want me to call or go get him?"

"Go get him! And get the one of the two Mounties on watch to assist. I cleared it with Inspector Smith. Get going, this is time sensitive!"

***

Thirty minutes later, Tom arrived at Gerber's house on Fig Tree Way. He parked just behind the Mounties' car and got out and walked up to a window. "Did you get the word that one of you is to accompany me to the door?" They both nodded in the affirmative. "OK, one of you come with me. I'm going to tell him to follow me to the office and I'd like you to follow, just in case he decides to go somewhere else."

"Sounds good."

The sidewalk side Mountie got out of the car and walked with Tom down the street to Gerber's house. Tom rang the doorbell and the door was opened my Jacqueline Mendes. "Ms. Mendes, is Mr. Gerber available?" asked Tom. She nodded yes and opened the door for them to come into the vestibule.

"Harry, the door is for you," called out Mendes.

"Who is it?"

"It is an auditor from the CRA that came with the search warrant and...." she looked at the constable who told her who he was "and a constable from the RCMP."

A few seconds later Gerber appeared. "Can't you people leave me alone? I was audited some time ago and they found nothing wrong!"

"No quite," replied Tom, "what the audit found was that your income couldn't be verified; the companies you said you worked for don't exist; and that after significant effort your income could not be verified. So, the file was referred to my unit, Special Investigations, to pursue. We have somewhat broader powers than the normal auditors and have the ability to demand information from various sources, plus work with the RCMP and federal prosecutors. So, if you'd please get your car keys and wallet, I'd like you to follow me to our office where we have some questions, we'd like to ask you."

"And what if I don't want to?" offered a defiant Gerber.

Before Tom could respond, the constable offered in a somewhat heavy-handed manner, "*Then sir*, I'd be pleased to offer you a chauffeur driven ride in my car."

Gerber shook his head, kissed Jacqueline and went to the garage. He pushed the garage door opener and got in his car.

CHAPTER 21

When they arrived at the CRA's office, Tom showed Gerber into the office, thanked the constables and released them from their duty. They rode the elevator to the fourth floor in silence.

When they got out, Tom led Gerber to the meeting room. Already there were Tom's boss and the sergeant from the criminal investigation branch. There was a large file on the table. Tom showed Gerber where to sit and moved to the opposite side of the table where he sat with his boss; the sergeant took a seat at the side of the table. After introductions, the interview began. Tom noted that it was being taped so that they didn't have to take notes.

Tom began, "Mr. Gerber, during an initial audit eighteen months ago, you denied that a signature on a purchase agreement for the car you drove here today was yours, and the auditor at that time was unable to confirm any of your declared sources of income or expenses. With the help of an auditor who was conducting a business audit, he did find out that that company leases four vehicles from a company we now know that you control."

"I don't know where you're getting this crap. I told that auditor the signature wasn't mine and that I didn't know anything about any trucks."

Tom continued, "We have since found that the company you control—Mambrino—I think it's called, if memory serves (feigning sorting through files)—yes that's right, just has client companies pay it the net amount. Now that amount goes to a post office box at a UPS store in the name of Mambrino, and your signature is on the rental agreement. We are in the process of getting copies of the documentation from those companies for the past two years at least, and maybe more." Gerber sat motionless, arms crossed, head down, with a scowl on his face. "Further, we found a courier company in Tillsonburg that uses vans purchased by Mambrino and with the company's logo on it. It is currently under audit by our London office.

"We also found information that indicates you have a bank account with the Third Manhattan Bank of New York, we found a partial bank account statement for that bank, and we found a credit card statement that shows flights and hotels in New York City that coincide with the deposits to that account—"

"All circumstantial," interjected Gerber.

"True, but after the search of your house—even though it is Ms. Mendes' name—you live there, we have found a substantial amount of records for Mambrino, along with bank statements from the New York bank as well as corporate credit card statements in Mambrino's name, and according to the TD Bank, you are the signing officer. And, by the way, the Minister of National Revenue has asked his counterpart at the US Internal Revenue Service to obtain details of that New York bank account, as well as other accounts or business you or your company might have with it."

"None of the government's business. Your search was an invasion of privacy. I'll sue you and this lousy government."

"Hold on now," interjected the sergeant, "Mr. Thomas hasn't come to the good part yet."

"That's right. During the search, one of the constables found a hidden panel in the wainscoting in the dining room. Behind it was a wall safe with a biometric lock. Ms. Mendes was very surprised, she said redoing the dining room was your idea. We asked her to try her fingerprints, but hers didn't work. Now, that safe has a place for two keys to be inserted and they have to be turned simultaneously. I guess a precaution in case something happens to the owner. Anyway, it took a while, but a constable found the keys hidden away in the cabinet in the garage. Do you know what we found when we opened the safe?"

Gerber sat silently, head down, saying nothing.

"We found $75,000 in various denominations, a bag of jewels, and, wait for it, an American passport in the name of Warren White, but with your picture. Amazing. And you sit there and tell us you know nothing about this?"

"I told the other auditor and I'm telling you; I know nothing about any of this—the trucks, the bank accounts, the box office, nothing. I'm being set up."

"By whom?" asked the sergeant "It would appear someone is going to a lot of trouble to frame you."

"I don't know, but I tell you those aren't my signatures."

"Well now," replied the sergeant, "I wouldn't be too sure of that. We sent copies of the purchase agreements for the trucks, vans and cars to our head office in Ottawa for a detailed handwriting analysis. And guess what? Don't want to guess? Ah, no comment, eh? Anyway, the signatures match yours on the tax returns you were forced to file. Are you going to tell us those are fake too?"

"You have no right to go through my house, to upset my girlfriend. What I do is my business and no one else's," Gerber spat out, looking at each in turn, "Not the CRA's, not RCMP's, not the government's. I'm just making a living."

"Is that an admission of guilt?" asked Tom.

"No, I'm not guilty of anything. The government forces honest folks, just out to make a living, to pay taxes, and for what I ask you? To give money to losers, like Bombardier, to keep jobs in shipyards when we could buy ships we need cheaper offshore, so the PM can take expensive trips and government ministers live high off the hog, and party faithful get cushy jobs in the Senate. Not my government."

Tom said softly, "If that's your concern, then there are more legitimate ways to object."

"I am objecting, I'm not using any of my money to fund those arseholes in Ottawa!"

Tom's boss now interjected, for the first time, "Mr. Gerber, we know for a fact that you were, in your own words, one of those 'arseholes'. You have a master's in economics and you lectured in taxation at a university. As Mr. Thomas said, we're working through the documents we collected from the house, the RCMP are going to have the jewels appraised, and we're getting information from the IRS. We don't yet know how you moved money out of Canada or how you got it in, but rest assured we will. We have very good people and Tom here is one of our best. And since it appears this is more than just simple tax evasion, but an elaborate scheme, you may face criminal prosecution. Do you understand?"

Gerber just shook his head. "So unfair, so unfair."

The sergeant then said, "Mr. Gerber, I'm going to ask you, informally, if you would please surrender your passport to me? I'm afraid from my point of view you are a potential flight risk, and we can't have that, can we? I'd also like Ms. Mendes'. Even though there is no evidence she is involved, she lives with you and could be coerced into perhaps doing something she wouldn't otherwise do. After all, you do go to New York a lot, or so it seems, and it isn't beyond reason that she might have accompanied you, even though she might not have known the actual purpose of the trip."

"And what if I say *no?* You have no right to take my passport!"

"Well, the folks back at the post are in the process of preparing a request to the court that, under the circumstances—what with you under investigation for tax fraud and who knows what else might turn up—that you are a potential flight risk and we want you to stay nearby...." looking at his watch, "In fact an Assistant Crown Attorney should be at the post right now, going over the request to the court and then heading off to the courthouse to make the submission. Now do you really want that on your record, that you were forced to surrender your passport? And that of Ms. Mendes."

Gerber sighed, "OK, OK, don't make a federal case out of it. If I can use my phone, I'll call her and ask her to have them out. I can bring them back—where, here or to your offices?"

"I wouldn't want to trouble you. I'll just follow you down, pick them up and give you a receipt."

"All right," responded a dejected Gerber.

While Gerber was on the phone to his girlfriend, the sergeant called the inspector and asked him to hold off on the request.

★★★

Tom's boss told him to get things organized as the following week would be both busy and boring, and then take the rest of the day off. So, Tom got a team of auditors together and planned to start going through the boxes from Gerber's house, starting on Monday morning.

"OK, ladies and gentlemen, what we are looking for is the following: 1) proof of payments from the companies we know the trucks were leased to, this could be a cheque stub or invoice from his company, Mambrino; 2) copies of his corporate credit card statements; 3) bank statements from the Third Manhattan Bank of New York; 4) records of travel to New York City or other places; 5) any Canadian bank accounts in his name or Mambrino's; 6) we know he has a passport in the name of Warren White so if you find anything with that name, set it aside and let me know; 7) anything that shows him getting US currency or travellers cheques or other types of funds that could be easily converted to US dollars; and finally, if you find anything you think is of interest, show me.

"Let me introduce, if you don't know her already, Margaret, the director's assistant. She will be coordinating your findings and putting them in date order. So, after you have found a few of the things we're looking for, please give them to her. She will log each item, along with who found it and then put it in date order as she gets more.

"As I said, this will be boring, so if you find you are getting tired and are afraid you might miss something, take a break, and then come back and join us. I hope we can get this done sooner than later, but it is important that we do this in as thorough a manner as possible to ensure we can reconstruct his income and his activities.

"Thank you, we'll reconvene here at eight-thirty Monday morning. Oh, and come dressed comfortably."

CHAPTER 22

Tom was in the office just after eight the following Monday. He was wearing faded blue jeans, golf shirt, and sneakers. Tom's boss saw him and said, "I see you're taking your own advice. Good choice, it's going to be a dirty job. How was your weekend?"

"Long and hard, boss, long and hard, but very enjoyable," replied Tom as he headed off to the room where the team would start going through boxes. His boss looked after him and shook his head, not understanding what Tom meant. It had rained all weekend so what could he have been doing that was so hard.

★★★

The team was all there by eight fifteen. Each took a box and as they found items of interest either passed them to Margaret to sort into categories, or to Tom for review. Time wore on through the morning as they went through box after box. Obviously, Gerber had no filing system, either intentionally or otherwise. As noon approached, Tom asked them what kind of pizzas they liked, noting that the director had authorized food so that they could eat as a group and discuss their findings in private.

After the pizzas arrived, they cleared the table of boxes and sat around and ate and talked. So far, they had come across eighteen months of credit card statements in the Mambrino company name. All showed expenses related to travel to New York City on a fairly regular basis, along with some meals and hotels, but not much of anything else. Of particular interest were charges for gasoline, purchased sometimes in Canada, but mostly in New York State, which they agreed meant that Gerber probably drove to New York City, or perhaps other locations in New York from time to time. But there were no charges for hotels other than New York City. Interestingly, the statements were stamped at various TD Bank branches, indicating that he had gone into the branches to pay the statements instead of paying online. And the statements were all addressed to the corporate mailbox address.

They had also found some statements from the various users of Mambrino's trucks that showed the amount of the payments made. But so far, they had not discovered any corresponding deposits to a bank account, business or personal.

After lunch, they spent another two hours going through boxes and then Tom suggested they go back to their desks and clean up anything that needed immediate attention and reconvene at 8:00 a.m. the next morning.

After everyone left, Tom went over what they found with Margaret and she set up spreadsheets for each category.

Tom got back to his own desk about four and checked his email. There was the normal administrative stuff, but one stood out. It was from Owen Charles and marked urgent. Tom headed over to Owen's desk and, finding him just getting ready to leave, said, "Hi Owen, what's so urgent?"

"Where have you been, Tom? I've been looking for you all afternoon!"

"I've been in a lock-up. We're going through Gerber's files."

"I found Warren White, or at least an Internet facsimile of him. While he has an Internet presence, he doesn't do social media, just follows various new outlets. But, of particular interest, I found a chatroom and a group called 'tax resister'. The members seem to think that the federal government should only collect excise taxes and nothing else. Now, according to this website, people can pay tax voluntarily, but only insofar as allocating it to a specific government program."

"What? How could the government possibly manage such a system?"

"Good question. The concept, in theory, would be like giving to a charity. The government would list its programs—say defence, healthcare, immigration, Aboriginal affairs, foreign aid, etc., and then individuals can allocate their income tax as they see fit. If a program doesn't get enough funding, it gets cut."

"Huh, democracy taken to the extreme," thought Tom out loud.

Owen went on, "Some of the comments are very, umm, how should I put it—disturbing in how they perceive ways to change the system. Also, I found that he has a bank account in New York City as well as investments there. Guess in whose name? No guess? In the name of Warren White!"

"Really! We knew he had a bank account, but we didn't have the number. And we wouldn't have found it because we were looking under Gerber. And he has investments too? You got the account numbers, Owen?

"Great work, Owen. I know you're heading home, but first thing tomorrow, send that information to the director, me and my boss. We've asked the IRS to check the bank in New York that we know of, but we thought the bank account was in Gerber's name. This should make the IRS's work easier. And you send it, I want the director to know who gets the credit for making this discovery. It might be a real breakthrough. Could you find a US social security number for him?"

"Thanks, Tom, I'll do it right now. I'll continue checking into White tomorrow and look for the social security number then." said Owen as he took off his jacket and booted up his computer again.

★★★

The next day, everyone was back in the room before 8:00 a.m. and going through boxes. A boring task, but as they went, they continued to build the story of Mambrino, more revenue, more charge card statements. Then, one of the junior auditors said, "Tom, look at this!" Tom looked. It was a receipt from an ATM that issued Bitcoins and gave an account number. Tom had been wondering how Gerber, aka White, got the money to New York. So maybe he converted cash into bitcoins and then got it out in New York. The Bitcoin market fluctuated, but maybe that was a cost of doing business. Unfortunately, they didn't know which name the account was in. And they didn't know how he converted the cheques Mambrino received from client companies into cash.

Tom said, "OK everyone, we now know that Gerber, or White as he is also known, converts cash into Bitcoin. I expected he then reconverts it in New York and deposits the cash into the bank there. Let's keep our eyes out for a receipt from someplace where he can cash cheques—like Western Union or Cash Converters."

"Just a minute," said the business auditor, "here, I just saw this and set it aside. It's a receipt from Western Union made out to Gerber. A year and a half ago he cashed a cheque in the amount of $18,552.82 at a Western Union branch. I was looking to see if there were others before saying anything."

"Great!" replied Tom, "Everyone, keep an eye out for similar receipts. If he was being really careful, I doubt he kept all the receipts. He may have kept some, either on purpose or by accident. I'm going to ask Owen Charles—the head of our tech group for those of you who don't know him—to see if he can trace the bitcoin account. Chinese OK for everyone for lunch?"

Getting positive nods, Tom headed out to find Owen and then order lunch.

CHAPTER 23

Tom took the ATM receipt for the cashed cheque to Owen Charles.

"Owen, can you get one of your people to try to track this account number? It is from an ATM that converts dollars into bitcoins. I'd like to know whose name is on the account."

"Will do, Tom."

Tom ordered lunch and then went back to his desk to check his email. He saw his boss heading towards him. "Tom, I was just coming to find you. The director wants to see us."

On the way to the director's office, Tom stuck his head in the room being used by the task force and asked Margaret to pick up the Chinese food when it arrived and pay for it. He was off to see the director.

"Tom, how's it going?" asked the director.

"Slowly sir, but we're making progress."

"Please call me Bob, we're a team." The director continued, "I got a call from Inspector Smith. They got back the appraisal on those diamonds and sapphires from the safe in Gerber's house. The appraised value is about five hundred thousand..." he let that hang in the air.

"Wow!" replied Tom and his boss simultaneously.

"So now, bring me up to date on what you've found so far."

"Well, we have found a smattering of proof of payment by the companies that lease the trucks, and from Mambrino's operation in Tillsonburg; we've got some credit card receipts in the company name that show fairly regular travel between Toronto and New York, and sometimes by car, sometimes by plane; one receipt has been found from a Western Union branch for a cashed cheque—the team is now looking for more—and we found a receipt from an ATM that converts cash into bitcoin. I've asked Owen Charles to try to track the receipt."

"So, what's the working theory?"

"We think that the companies and the Tillsonburg operation send the net revenue to the box office at the UPS store. Gerber picks these up and goes to a cheque-cashing store. We found a Western Union receipt, but he probably uses others. He then goes to the ATM, maybe keeps some cash for himself and then deposits it and buys some Bitcoin. He does this for a while and then goes to New York where he redeems the Bitcoin for cash and then deposits that in the account there and comes home. Maybe with some variations on the theme, but that's what I'm thinking right now."

"Good. I follow your reasoning and it seems sound. Try to tie it down. I'll get on to the IRS with the account information Owen Charles found—he's a smart cookie, isn't he?"

Tom and his boss left the director's office and Tom invited him to the room the team was using for lunch and to sit in on the brainstorming.

***

By the end of the day Wednesday, the team had gone through all the boxes taken from Gerber's house. Tom suggested they reconvene mid-morning on Thursday and take another look through the boxes just in case they missed something. But most of the non-tax-related material had been sorted into separate boxes, so it was simply a matter of scanning through that material to see if anything had been missed, now that they knew exactly what they were looking for. That process resulted in finding a few more remittances from the client companies, but a major find was an envelope that contained receipts for Bitcoin purchases that totaled close to $500,000. The envelope was undated and unremarkable in any way so it was easy to understand why it had initially been overlooked as it was in a stack of other envelopes that contained things like gas and car maintenance receipts.

Tom reported to the director that they had gone through all the boxes' contents and now the material found needed to be sorted into date order and tallied. While Margaret had done an excellent job in sorting the documents into a spreadsheet sorted by type and date, if known, it wasn't her job to perform an audit function, such as which, if any, of the expenses were actually allowable for tax purposes.

The director told Tom to tell the team to take Friday off, without having to use vacation days and to thank them for their help. Tom was to do the same, although he declined as he wanted to get a start on going through the revenue sources.

CHAPTER 24

By the middle of the following week, Tom had an idea of Gerber's, aka Mambrino's, revenue for each of the past three years. Revenue from earlier was hard to determine as not many remittance slips had been found. Even for the years that Tom had a good idea of revenue, there were gaps. As a general rule, each client company and the courier company had mailed remittances—cheques—monthly to the Mambrino mailbox. So, for each year there should be 36 remittances, but in point of fact, these ranged from 28 for the earliest year to 35 for the last year reviewed. Tom hoped that the material requested from the client companies, and from the audit of the courier company, would fill out the details and maybe even take the unreported back another year or two.

The end of the week brought some good news. Copies of cheques and the accompanying remittance forms from the two client companies helped to fill out the three years, as well as providing detailed revenue information on Mambrino for the previous seven years. With the exception of the most current year, four of those years overlapped the years that he had been forced to file personal tax returns. In addition, there were five previous years of unreported income.

So, the returns that had been filed as a result of court action were nothing but pure works of fiction. That, coupled with the New York account and investment information, started to lead Tom to the conclusion that he was now dealing not only with a case of tax evasion, but tax fraud as well.

With that information in hand, along with what they had found going through the files they had seized from Gerber's residence, Tom set to work piecing together the revenue picture from Mambrino's operations.

He used the spreadsheet that the director's assistant, Margaret, had used. He inserted each company's revenue and found he had to add columns as it turned out he had ten years' worth of data. In total, the unreported revenue amount to $3.3 million. More in the last five years and less in the first five. Tom figured this was due to the loans to finance the vehicle purchases, which had been paid off during the first five, plus the fact that the courier company had only been set up four years previous. So far, they had found about $575,000 in cash and jewels. And they knew about the US bank account, which had a current balance of USD $271,560, which roughly equated to CAD $350,000. The valuator from the London office, Sandra McLean, had estimated the value of collectables in the Fig Tree way property at about $750,000, but that was a current estimate and may not represent the purchase price. And, there was apparently an investment account at the New York Bank. Was there more?

Tom went to his boss's cubicle and updated him.

"Good work, Tom. Did you ever confirm the total amount of the mortgage held on house?"

"No, I just confirmed the mortgage was held by the Overland Bank and Trust Company. OK boss, I know we need to tie down where that income went. I know there are works of art in the house, so some probably is hanging on the walls. In addition, I assume he made some investment income. We'll know about that when we get the US bank and investment statements."

CHAPTER 25

On the following Monday, Tom went to the branch of the Overland Bank and Trust Company that Jacqueline Mendes dealt with, identified himself, and asked to speak to the manager.

"I'd like to see the account for this mortgage, held by Ms. Jacqueline Mendes on 52 Fig Tree Way, please."

"I'm sorry," replied the manager, "I can't do that without either permission from Ms. Mendes or you need to provide a Demand for Information. It's bank policy not to allow access to client records without proper authorization."

"May I use your phone?" asked Tom.

"Certainly."

Tom looked at his notes on his cell phone and dialed a number. "Ms. Mendes? Hello, it's Tom Thomas from the CRA calling." Tom continued, "I'm at your bank… yes, the Overland Bank and Trust Company. I need to take a look at your mortgage records, specifically the opening balance and the payments that have been made to date. Do I have your permission…? Just a minute, I'll let you speak to the manager."

"This is Jacqueline Mendes, please let Mr. Thomas see any information he needs to review."

"May I have your client card number and date of birth? I just need to confirm it is in fact you," asked the manager. He looked up the information and then confirmed it was correct. "Mr. Thomas, just give me a minute, and I'll look up the information and print it for you."

Tom took the pages of mortgage payments, thanked the manager and headed back to the office.

The original purchase price of the house had been just under one million, and Mendes had put down a down payment of three hundred thousand, which presumably came from the net proceeds of the sale of hers and Gerber's previous residences. It was a 30-year mortgage with an initial annual interest rate of four per cent, resulting in a monthly payment of $3,500. While high, given Mendes reported income, she could afford it. And there had been an annual pre-payment of ten thousand each year and while Gerber may have made that—and that wasn't obvious from the payment records, it really didn't amount to much. He would have to talk to Jacqueline Mendes to be sure. But the collectibles and artwork were beyond her financial ability, based again on her reported income.

Tom picked up the phone, "Ms. Mendes, this is Tom Thomas. I've been going over your mortgage payments and I notice an annual prepayment of $10,000. Did you make those payments or did Mr. Gerber?"

"Harold gave me that money to put on the mortgage."

"I see, what about the monthly payments?"

"No, that was all my money. While we live together, we each keep our accounts separately, as I had told you."

"Sorry, I don't mean to question your integrity. Just one more question for now. Who bought the artwork and other collectibles in the house?"

"Harold bought most of them. But I bought the desk and I inherited a couple of paintings from my great-uncle when he died."

"Oh, when was that and can you give me an estimate of the value?"

"He died six years ago. He was an old bachelor and had quite an art collection along with other old items. He didn't trust banks so he invested in tangible assets, like art and antiques. He left everything to his great-nieces and nephews. I guess what I received was worth about a $250,000, based on the probated value of his will."

"How nice of him. You know a lot about probate and estates?"

"Yes, given my background he made me one of the executors of his estate."

"Would you mind giving me a list of which items you inherited and the approximate value then and today?"

"Well, I can give you the value when I inherited them, but I've got no idea what the value is today, and I don't want to hire an appraiser."

"I understand," replied Tom, "the value when you inherited the items would be fine."

While the value of what Mendes had inherited was about $250,000 that still left $500,000 unaccounted for, in terms of present value. But she didn't know the current value, so the actual value Gerber had contributed was unknown. Tom emailed Sandra McLean to see if she could come to town again. He figured that if Ms. Mendes could tell her the items she inherited, that Sandra could provide an estimated market value. While that would further reduce the discrepancy in value, it still wouldn't tell what Gerber had paid.

Tom knew it was important to, so far as possible, detail where the unreported revenue had gone so that any defence questioning the revenue figure could be substantiated by showing where the money went. It was a tough job, but worth the effort, given that it was now known that Gerber would try to lie his way out of any assessment or, in the case of the four returns that were filed, reassessment.

CHAPTER 26

The following week, Sandra McLean came to Kitchener and met with Jacqueline Mendes and Tom. She took a look at the items Mendes inherited, took photos and told Tom she would get back to him once she had an estimated value.

That week also brought news from the IRS. They had obtained the bank records from New York as well as White's investment account. In addition, they had determined he had a safe deposit box, and with the appropriate pressure on the bank manager had accessed that as well.

The bank account had been opened eight years ago, and while the balance went up and down, most of the withdrawals could be traced to the deposits in the investment account, which had a current market value of about $500,000. The amount invested, over time, amounted to $322,525. So, there was more revenue that could be traced. But the safe deposit box was the surprise, it contained loose diamonds and gold jewellery, which the IRS estimated was worth another $500,000. All figures were, of course, in US dollars.

After sharing this information with his boss, Tom set to work reconciling the known revenue to the known assets, as well as reviewing known expenditures, which were related to the charge card they had discovered.

The next day Tom walked into his boss's cubicle.

"Based on the verification of revenue to Mambrino we received, I make the total revenue at $3.3 million over the ten-year period we have information for. In the earlier years, it was a little lower as the client companies were actually paying off the loans to purchase the trucks. In terms of where that money has gone, I've determined that we can account for roughly $3,398,144. So, some of this is investment income and doesn't account for money Gerber has spent. This figure would also be dependent on the actual exchange rate at the time the funds were transferred to the US account and, as well, as I said, there is some investment income included in that figure."

"Break it down for me, Tom."

"OK, for the US funds I assumed an average exchange rate of twenty-five per cent. In terms of US assets, we've got $322,525 in an investment account; diamonds from the safe deposit box with an estimated market value of $500,000; and, $271,000 in the bank account, for a total of $1,093,525 US. Using the twenty-five per cent exchange rate estimate, that's about $1,366,906 Canadian. Then we found $590,500 worth of stuff in the safe in the house. This is comprised of $75,000 in cash, $15,500 in money orders and diamonds and sapphires with an estimated market value of $500,000. In addition, going through the company's credit statement I found travel expenses, which is all the card was used for, to and from New York City, of $15,545.82."

"Great work, Tom. Now the payments were to the company, correct?"

"Yes, but the US accounts were in White's, aka Gerber's, name only."

"So, do we assess the company or him?" pondered Tom's boss.

"Good question. I guess we could assess the company for the unreported income and then allow a deduction for the income deposited by Gerber aka White. It is an interesting issue as it seems that Gerber just cashed the cheques and then took the money. So, maybe we can argue the company is a sham. After all, we've found no proof it actually existed. And since it never existed and Gerber took the funds for himself. I think we can assess Gerber personally for it all."

"Interesting thought. I think we need to talk to the director as we've got a tax fraud issue as well. We also have the issue of the phony US passport. We'll have to talk to our RCMP friends as well about what criminal charges that might entail."

CHAPTER 27

Two days later, Tom and his boss walked into the boardroom beside the director's office. Seated around the table were the director along with the RCMP Inspector Smith and a woman they didn't know. The latter was introduced as Samantha Yang, an Assistant Crown Attorney. The discussion was straightforward: Mr. Gerber would be charged with filing fraudulent tax returns in respect of the previous four years of returns filed as a result of the court order. In addition, he would be charged with not filing income tax returns for the past seven years, for a total amount of unreported income over that time of $2,310,000. This amount was supported by the amounts they could prove he received from the various companies he provided services to. He would be assessed personally on the basis that his corporation had not filed tax returns, and in fact they could find no proof it had ever been registered. He had personally picked up the cheques. In addition, he would be assessed Harmonized Sales Tax of $300,300 as he was providing business services as a self-employed individual. In addition to the total amount, interest and penalties would also be assessed. These would add approximately fifty per cent to the estimated tax liability of approximately $1,174,000.

Then Samantha Yang stated: "Gerber will also be charged separately with money laundering, with respect to the money moved to the American account using Bitcoin. In addition, he will also be criminally charged with tax fraud. These latter two charges would be handled by the criminal division of the Crown Attorney's office." Looking towards Inspector Smith, she went on, "I'll contact one of my colleagues in the Criminal Division and ask for a warrant to be issued for Mr. Gerber's arrest. The charges will be money laundering and the use of a false passport in a criminal enterprise. Correct?"

The inspector nodded.

"Good. I'll have them email a copy to your office and then send the original by courier. You can go ahead with the arrest once you receive them."

It was then agreed that Mr. Gerber would be invited to come into the Frederick Street office on the following Friday, to discuss the findings of the CRA audit.

Then the RCMP would wait for Gerber at his home and arrest him there.

When Tom got back to his cubicle, he phoned the house on Fig Tree Way.

"Hello," answered the feminine voice on the other end of the line.

"Ms. Mendes, this is Tom Thomas. Is Mr. Gerber at home? I'd like to speak to him."

"Yes, he's just getting ready to go away for a few days. I'll get him."

"Hello, this is Harold Gerber. What do you want now!"

"Mr. Gerber. I understand you are getting ready to go away for a few days. Where are you going?"

"None of your business."

"I have completed the audit of your business interests and unreported income. I want to meet with you to go over the results. Friday was what I was thinking of, but if you are unavailable then, we can simply issue the assessment. However, I would really like to meet with you and give you a chance to respond before finalizing our findings. You are to be in our office at 9:00 a.m. this Friday, the day after tomorrow, or we will simply issue the assessment without any chance for you to respond."

There was silence on the end of the phone and then, finally, Gerber spoke. "Fine. I'll postpone my trip. I was going to visit my parents, who live in Saskatchewan. But I can go later."

On Friday, Gerber presented himself at the appointed time and was led to the conference room by a clerical staff person. There he was met by Tom and his boss. "Mr. Gerber, we've completed the assessment of your income for the past ten years, however we can only charge you with unreported income for the past seven years. Now, we have, based on information received from various sources, including the companies your transports did business with, the unreported income for the past ten years is just over $3.3 million. For the past seven years that results in unreported income of $2,310,000. In addition, as the company, Mambrino, that supposedly conducted this business appears to be unregistered and never filed tax returns, we are assessing you personally with this income—"

Gerber started to object, but Thomas continued, "and in addition—*and in addition*—you are being assessed with not remitting $300,300 in HST."

"That's absolutely *ridiculous!*"

"Well sir, the facts dispute that. We have gone through the remittances we received from the various companies and your courier business. And we have proved much of that income, if not more, through expenses that are attributable to you, along with the money and jewels found in the safe in your home and the investments in the Third Manhattan Bank of New York. I should also tell you that penalties and interest will be assessed, but that is beyond our scope to discuss in detail."

Gerber interrupted again, "What do you mean penalties and interest? I don't believe in paying taxes that I can't agree with or say how the money is used. So, you got me. That's it."

"Not at all, sir. You will be charged penalties for failing to file tax returns, and, in addition, under the Act you will be charged interest from the date the tax for each year should have been paid, along with interest on the appropriate HST that should have been paid for each year. As well, you filed false tax returns for four of the years we investigated. You will also be charged with tax fraud for filing fraudulent tax returns."

"So how much are you going to screw me over for?" snarled Gerber.

"Well, we don't assess either interest or penalties at this level. We simply issue an assessment for the amount of unreported income and sales tax. Another group will calculate the interest and penalties based on the law and the interest rates that were in force for each of the years audited. The amount owing, based on the unreported income and unpaid HST, I'd estimate about $1,174,000 and so the interest and penalties will probably add another fifty per cent to that, or say between five hundred and seven hundred thousand dollars. So, I think you should plan on finding about two million dollars. I should also inform you that in addition to financial penalties you could also be subject to a prison term. But that will be up to the judge to determine, should you decide to appeal.

"Once you receive the Notice of Assessment you have the right to appeal the findings either through an administrative procedure or the Tax Court of Canada. There you can either do an informal appeal, from which you can appeal no further. Or, you can do a formal process, following the full rules of procedure, which might allow you to appeal further to the Federal Court. However, you should be aware that while you have these avenues available to you, unless you pay the amount assessed initially, interest will continue to accrue until you either pay it or the assessment is overturned or reduced. If you do pay immediately and are entitled to a refund, that refund will have interest paid to you.

"Finally, given the seriousness of these offences with which you are charged, I strongly recommend you seek legal counsel. Do you have any questions?"

"You're nothing but bureaucratic thugs forcing people to pay money to a government that spends money like it's its own, not the people's. No, I disagree with tax for tax sake. And yes, I'll get a lawyer, a good one, who can make my case in court. You wait and see!" and Gerber stormed out of the room.

Gerber was as mad as hell and he headed to his parked car. He checked his watch and noted the bars wouldn't be open yet, so he headed home and decided he'd have a couple of drinks and then, when he calmed down, find out how to find legal counsel—something he had never thought he'd need.

As he turned onto Fig Tree Way, he noted a silver-grey Ford with two men sitting in it. His antenna was heightened, and he wondered what they were doing there. As he turned into his driveway, he noticed the Ford coast to a stop in front of his house. A man and a woman got out of the car and walked towards him. He stopped.

"Mr. Gerber?"

"Yes."

"Mr. Gerber, I'm Sergeant Knowles, this is Constable Shantz. We're with the RCMP. We are here to arrest you on the charges of money laundering and using a false identity, specifically a false United States passport. It is my duty to inform you that you have the right to retain and instruct counsel without delay. You may call any lawyer you want. There is a 24-hour telephone service available, which provides a legal aid duty lawyer who can give you legal advice in private. This advice is given without charge and the lawyer can explain the legal aid plan to you. If you wish to contact a legal aid duty lawyer, I can provide you with a telephone number. Do you understand? Do you want to call a lawyer? You are not obliged to say anything, but anything you do say may be given in evidence in court."

Gerber snarked, "That's not what they say on cop shows!"

"That's American TV, sir. Please come with us."

A dejected Gerber replied, "Can I at least say good-bye to my girlfriend and get some personal effects?"

"You can say good-bye to her. We will accompany you. We will inform Ms. Mendes later as to where you are so she can bring you some things. You will also be able to talk with her at some point and you can tell her what else you need."

After saying good-bye to Jacqueline, he was placed in handcuffs and put in the back seat of the cruiser and driven away. Mendes was left in tears on the front step.

PART 2

CHAPTER 28

SATURDAY MORNING

After having spent the Friday night in RCMP custody and having been given the opportunity to contact legal aid, he was taken to the Kitchener courthouse for an 11:00 am appearance.

"Mr. Gerber, you are charged with money laundering and having and using a false passport in another name and in the name of another country, namely the United States of America. How do you plead?" asked Madam Justice Lucinda LeGrande.

"Madam Justice, I'm Christopher Lee from legal aid. Mr. Gerber was only arrested and charged yesterday. He has no legal counsel of his own—at least with respect to criminal proceedings and he needs time to find a full-time criminal attorney who can address the charges against him. He therefore needs to be able to use the telephone and perhaps visit various attorneys until he finds one suitable. I also understand that the Canada Revenue Agency will be charging him with tax evasion, and he will need to find appropriate legal counsel for that charge. On that basis, I ask he be released on his own recognizance for a period of time, say one week, in order for him to accomplish this. Until permanent representation is found my client declines to enter a plea at this time."

"Mr. Lee, will you or your office be assisting him in this endeavour?"

"Yes, Your Honour, we will be."

"Madam Justice, if I may?"

"Go ahead, Mr. Lougheed" instructed Justice LeGrande.

"While I appreciate my colleague's desire that his client have the opportunity to find appropriate counsel to defend him, I would note that these are serious charges. In addition, he faces charges of evading tax of about $1.7 million plus another $300 thousand in HST. That excludes any interest or penalties on that charge. Not to mention, if convicted, he could face a prison term. So, I can't just let him walk out of the court and assume he'll return of his own volition."

"What do you propose, Mr. Lougheed?"

"I'd like the court to impose bail in the amount of $500,000 to ensure Mr. Gerber appears, and I'd appreciate Your Honour setting a date for his next appearance."

"I can appreciate my learned counsel's concern," interjected Mr. Yang. "However, my client doesn't have that level of funds currently available, given the assessment by the CRA against him. I also appreciate he would like a firm date for his next appearance. In the alternative, I would suggest that Mr. Gerber be fitted with an ankle bracelet that allows him to go to meetings within the boundaries of Waterloo Region in order to retain legal counsel."

"Mr. Lougheed, what do you say?" asked Justice LeGrande.

"The Crown finds that satisfactory, Your Honour. I would also ask that Your Honour schedule the next hearing no longer than next Friday morning."

"Point taken, Mr. Lougheed. So ordered. Mr. Gerber, the Crown has been more generous than you might otherwise have expected. You have until 10:00 a.m. next Friday to find and retain legal counsel. If you do not appear at that time, I will issue a bench warrant for your arrest and on my authority, you will be held without bail until your trial date. Do you understand?"

"Yes, Your Honour. Thank you very much."

CHAPTER 29

Promptly, at ten, the following Friday morning Harold Gerber again appeared before Madam Justice LeGrande.

"Mr. Gerber, how nice to see you today."

"Thank you, Your Honour."

"Madam Justice, I'm Samuel L. Brock. I'll be representing Mr. Gerber for the balance of these proceedings."

"Madam Justice, I'm Associate Crown Counsel Trevor Harris for the Crown."

"Mr. Brock, Mr. Harris, you have both appeared before me in the past. Mr. Brock, how does your client plead?"

"Not guilty, Your Honour," responded Gerber.

"Mr. Harris, what say you on bail?"

"Your Honour, I have been in touch with a collogue, Samantha Yang, who will be handling Mr. Gerber's prosecution with respect to his tax evasion case and the unpaid taxes. I now have a better idea of what he is facing. The Crown still feels that due to the facts in this case that a significant financial incentive is required."

"Your Honour, if I may?"

"Yes, Mr. Brock?"

"Mr. Gerber and I have talked to his girlfriend, Ms. Mendes, with whom he cohabitates. They are in the process of selling their house and buying another in New Hamburg. Ms. Mendes has agreed to take a portion of the sale proceeds, and use a loan until the closing, to secure bond for Mr. Gerber."

"Is this generous lady in the court?" enquired Justice LeGrande.

"I am, Your Honour," responded Jacqueline Mendes as she stood.

"Ms. Mendes, you must love the accused very much? What is the value of the home you are selling?"

"We will be receiving $1.7 million on closing, a week from next Monday," responded Mendes.

"And the cost of your new house?"

"About $1.2 million. It's a little farther from Kitchener, but I work from home, as does Harold. And I'm hoping we can invest the difference in a home in Arizona for the winter as we would like to retire earlier than later."

"The Crown has requested a surety of $500 thousand in the event Mr. Gerber does not comply with his bail conditions. Are you willing to do so?"

"What does that mean, Your Honour?"

"Unlike our neighbours to the south, in Canada we don't have a bail system. Rather, we either release someone on their own recognizance or ask a third party to provide a surety, or guarantee, that the accused will appear for trial and not otherwise violate any terms of bail. In this case, the surety would be that you would sign a promissory note to the court in the amount of $500 thousand. That means that if Mr. Gerber violates any terms of his release, such as leaving the country or province without permission of the court, or fails to appear at a scheduled court hearing, you would have to pay the court the amount of the promissory note. Do you understand, Ms. Mendes?"

"Yes, Your Honour. I'm willing to do this if it means Harold, I mean Mr. Gerber, can come home with me."

"So ordered," stated Madam Justice LeGrande. "Any other business?"

"Your Honour, if I may?"

"Yes, Mr. Brock?"

"Before he was arrested, Mr. Gerber was planning on going to Saskatchewan to visit his parents. They are in their late seventies and his mother has not been well. The defence would appreciate it if the bail requirement to remain in Waterloo Region be modified so that he can visit his parents within the next week, for a period of three days. Further, we would ask that, with prior notice to the court and with the court's approval, Mr. Gerber could visit his parents again, especially if his mother's health deteriorates."

"Mr. Gerber. I have empathy for your situation. However, this is a court of law. I will allow you to visit your parents within the next week, for a period not exceeding four days. You must notify the Crown Counsel's office as well as Mr. Brock and provide copies of your travel documents, airline tickets and where you are staying while in Saskatchewan. You must provide this information in person twenty-four hours prior to leaving. The only exception will be in the event of a death, in which case a copy of the death certificate must also be provided on your return. You may fax or email your travel arrangements in that case. But *only* in that case.

"You obviously have a woman who loves you very much if she is willing to put up $500 thousand as a surety for you. Don't abuse her trust.

"Anything further, gentlemen?"

"No, Your Honour"

"No, Your Honour."

"Fine, one final piece of business. Counsels, please have your list of witnesses and anticipated timeline to the Clerk within the next 60 days and then a trial date will be set. Adjourned!"

CHAPTER 30

A week later, Harold Gerber received the Notice of Assessment from the CRA with respect to his unreported income for the past seven years and a day later the one arrived for the amount of Harmonized Sales Tax that was due on the unreported business income.

In total, the amount of tax owing was $1,174,635, of which $135,135 was for the unremitted HST. In addition, penalties and interest on both were in excess of $587,000. The assessments noted that if the amounts owing were not paid within 30 days, interest would continue to accrue.

He was also advised in a separate covering letter that he had 90 days to appeal the assessments.

"Can I speak with Mr. MacPharland, please?" asked Gerber when he called the tax lawyer's office that had been recommended to him.

"Who's calling please?" asked a polite female voice.

"My name is Harold Gerber. Mr. MacPharland was recommended to me by Samuel Brock, who is representing me in another case."

"Mr. MacPharland is currently on the phone and will be in court for the rest of the day. Would you like to make an appointment to speak with him? You could bring in the information you have and discuss your situation in detail. Mr. MacPharland doesn't charge for a consultation, and he can determine what he can do for you."

"Fine! When is the earliest I can see him?"

"He has time Thursday morning, the day after tomorrow, at 10:00 a.m."

"OK. I'll bring in the Notices of Assessment then. If he has time, you might ask him to call Samuel Brock beforehand so he has some information on that case, as both are related."

"I'll give him a note to do that with your name. Have a nice rest of your day, sir."

'Have a nice rest of your day,' fumed Gerber, *Oh well, she doesn't know what's happening and is just doing her job. Have a nice day indeed! I need a scotch!*

CHAPTER 31

At nine forty-five on Thursday morning, he walked into the offices of Zive, MacPharland and Kromesky. "Hello, I'm Harold Gerber. I've got an appointment with Mr. MacPharland at ten o'clock."

"Oh yes, Mr. Gerber. I'll call him and let him know you're here," replied the lithe young lady behind the reception counter.

A few minutes later a tall, rather rotund, gentleman with dark hair, greying at the temples, came out of a corridor. "Mr. Gerber. I'm Mark MacPharland, come back to my office and I'll see what we can do for you." He was dressed more casually than Gerber, wearing herringbone sports jacket and slacks, whereas Gerber had come in a dark suit and tie—thinking it would make him look more business-like.

"Mr. MacPharland, I've got a problem—two actually," started Harold Gerber, "I've been charged with not paying income tax and HST for the past seven years. In addition, I've been charged in a separate case with money laundering and using a false passport. I need help!"

"Yes, you do, sir. Can you tell me what on earth you were thinking! I've spoken with Mr. Brock and learned about your tax problem. But using a false passport and sending money offshore. What on earth were you thinking!"

"Well, you see, I'm against paying income tax that goes towards government programs or expenses that I don't agree with."

"You mean you're a tax denier?"

"No, no, not at all. I know the government has the power to levy income tax, but I want to have a say in where and how my tax dollars are spent. Not leave it up to a bunch of elected nincompoops who are looking out for the interests of businesses that support them."

"Well, this isn't the United States you know, where elected officials are beholding to powerful lobbyists."

"Yes, I know that. At least in theory. But instead of spending money wisely and saving money, we support industries that would not otherwise be competitive if the government didn't give them overpriced contracts or want offsetting industrial benefits when we do give government contracts to foreign contractors."

"But isn't that way the government does business? Why do you get to tell it how to do business?"

"Are you going to help me or are you on 'their' side!" demanded a defiant Harold Gerber.

"Hold on, Mr. Gerber. I'm just illustrating the types of questions you will be asked. You need to explain yourself using specific examples. And I'm not saying we will win but given your passion, I think it would be appropriate to give you a forum to express your concerns. And I think those concerns might be felt by a number of Canadians who are concerned about a growing national debt and lack of government action on a number of fronts."

"So, you'll take my case?"

"Yes, but don't hold out a lot of hope about winning and getting the assessment reversed. If you can, I suggest you pay as much, if not all, of the amounts you have been assessed. If not, the interest will continue to grow. If we win, which I doubt, you'll get a refund. But I promise I'll do my best to give you a forum to express your views."

"Thank you, sir. What do you need from me?"

CHAPTER 32

The following Monday, Harold was in the offices of his criminal attorney, Samuel L. Brock. His tax attorney, Mark MacPharland was also in attendance.

"Well, Mr. Gerber, to paraphrase a song, 'you got troubles'. Whatever possessed you to acquire a false passport and open US investment and bank accounts?" enquired Mr. Brock, as he leaned back in his chair, steepled his hands, and looked over his half-glasses at his client.

Gerber reiterated what he had told Mark MacPharland.

"That's fine. You disagree with how the government spends the tax dollars it collects. But to reiterated Mr. Brock's question: what possessed you to obtain a false passport, move money to the US and open U.S. accounts in another name. And to buy diamonds to boot," asked MacPharland.

"That happened later. I had money that I couldn't hide easily. So, I thought if I got a false passport and moved money to the US it would be easier to hide."

"Really! You thought that was a good idea! It smacks of intent to evade tax and to launder money," stated Brock. "Tell me how you did it. And don't leave out anything."

"OK. I had built up some funds and didn't want to invest them in Canada. I used some to help my fiancée, Jacqueline Mendes, with her mortgage payments and I bought more trucks and cars, but that wasn't enough to use the money. If I invested it in Canada, I'd get tax slips and the government would know about the investment income and then might wonder where I got the capital. That's why I filed false tax returns initially—"

"After you were charged with failure to file returns," interrupted MacPharland.

"Yes, but I hoped they would at least provide some rationale for the money I had. Then, a couple of years ago, Jacqueline and I went to New York on a trip. I went out on my own one afternoon and visited some less than reputable bars—"

"How did you learn of those?" interrupted Brock.

"Ahh, I spoke with a guy in a strip club in Cambridge and he gave me a couple of names of bars where I might get help."

"About moving money out of Canada. Correct?"

"Yes. In any event, I eventually was referred who a guy to could acquire a US passport. It already had a name on it. All it needed was a picture. So, I went to a copy shop that did the photo and I gave it to this guy. I had the passport before we left New York. Simple really."

"And you used this when you went to the States?"

"No, no. I used my Canadian passport. I only used the US passport to open the accounts at the bank and I gave them a false address. I also got a fake social security number from the person I bought the passport from."

"So that when they mailed tax slips to you, you didn't get them."

"Correct, sir."

"Well, Mr. Gerber, this doesn't look good. You are charged with money laundering and using a false passport, which you have readily admitted to me. I don't see much of a defence," stated MacPharland

"But I did it because of my belief that Canadians should have some direct say in how they're tax dollars are spent. Doesn't that count for anything?"

After Harold Gerber left the meeting the two lawyers huddled.

"I don't really see any viable defence regarding the tax assessment," sighed Mark MacPharland.

"I agree," said Brock. "Maybe he should plead no contest to the tax assessment and then I just fight the evasion and fraud charges in federal court on the basis that he doesn't agree with the way the government spends money. Maybe I can find an expert witness that would testify along that line."

MacPharland agreed. "I know a professor at one of the local universities that lectures in tax, but he has made a specialty of looking at cases in the past that dealt with people resisting or finding ways not to pay taxes imposed by the government of the day."

"Fine. That's fine. Could you ask him to contact me? Maybe I can at least provide a rationale for our client's actions."

CHAPTER 33

The Office of Assistant Crown Attorney Trevor Harris

"Hi Samantha, come on in."

"Hi Trevor, what's up?"

"I got a call from Mark MacPharland late yesterday. He and Samuel Brock put their heads together after a joint meeting with Gerber. They have decided to have him plead guilty to the failure to remit income and sales taxes but intend to fight in federal court the tax evasion and fraud charges on the basis that he is a 'tax resister'. He apparently feels the public doesn't have enough say over the way government spends 'their' dollars."

"I've heard of them—a little different perspective from the 'deniers', but their position is untenable. Imagine if everyone who paid taxes had a say in how their taxes were spent? It would be a nightmare, both federally and provincially!"

"So, I'm out then as there is no tax trial."

"No, not at all. The boss wants you to sit second chair and handle the tax side of the prosecution, and I'll handle the criminal side."

"I thought they are agreeing to the tax assessment?"

"They are. But we need to build the case for evasion and fraud. One way to do that is to show the lengths he went to hide his income."

"Great. I'm looking forward to getting a crack at this character!"

CHAPTER 34

Five months later...

"All rise! Her Honour Barbara Laughlin presiding."

After Justice Laughlin took her seat she said, "OK, let's get started."

"Your Honour, Trevor Harris for the Crown, ably assisted by Ms. Samantha Yang ."

"Your Honour, Samuel L. Brock and Mark MacPharland for the defence."

"Does the defence agree to waive the reading of the charges?"

"Yes, Your Honour."

"Fine, how does your client plead?"

"Guilty to the charge of not filing tax returns or paying income and sales taxes for the years in question," stated Gerber, "But not guilty to the charges of tax evasion and money laundering, Your Honour."

"How can you plead guilty to one and not the other?" asked the judge.

"Your Honour," stated Samuel L. Brock, whilst clearing his throat. "The defence does not contest the unreported income; however, we intend to argue that Mr. Gerber had good reason for not filing returns and paying income tax."

"Hmmm, should prove interesting. Gentlemen, are you ready to proceed?"

"Yes, Your Honour," both replied in unison.

CHAPTER 35

"Mr. Harris, are you ready to proceed?"

"Yes, Your Honour. The Crown calls Ms. Sandra McLean."

For the next two hours, the CRA appraiser, under questioning by Samantha Yang, reviewed the collectables found in Gerber's home and their value, providing substantiation not only for the assessed unreported income, but also on Gerber's attempt to hide the unreported income by purchasing collectables. The Crown then called Al Edwards to the stand. At that point, the defence interrupted to object to the anticipated parade of witnesses that would substantiate the assessment of the unreported income on the basis that the defence had already stipulated that their client had pleaded no contest to the assessment, but was arguing that he did not illegally evade paying income tax. In response, the Crown argued that while the defendant had indeed stipulated to the unreported income, the purpose of this examination was to establish the lengths to which the defendant had gone to hide, and therefore, evade paying income and sales tax on his income. The judge agreed with the Crown's argument and allowed the line of question to continue after a break for lunch.

Al Edwards was called, the initial auditor who could neither prove nor disprove the income that the defendant had reported, after he had been taken to court for failure to file tax returns for several years. He was then followed by Tom Thomas, who described the Special Investigations unit's investigation in some detail. His testimony was interrupted at 5:00 p.m. and the judge said the court would reconvene at 8:00 a.m. the following Monday.

On the Monday, Thomas continued his very detailed testimony, including the finding of the US passport in the hidden safe and the subsequent discovery of how Gerber moved money to the United States and the accounts and investments there.

Following Thomas's testimony, Samantha Yang asked permission to read into the record a letter from the IRS agent who had visited the bank in New York City and discovered the bank account and investments held there in the name on the American passport.

The defence interrupted to say that it would stipulate to the contents of the letter, so there was no need for it to be read into the record. Ms. Yang agreed, so long as a copy was entered into evidence by giving it to Judge Laughlin. At that point, Judge Laughlin gave a copy to the court clerk.

On Tuesday, the Crown wrapped up its case by calling Sergeant Knowles of the RCMP to give his version of events regarding the finding of the hidden safe. Following his testimony, the Crown rested its case, subject to closing arguments.

"Mr. Brock, will you be ready to proceed with the defence tomorrow morning at nine-thirty?"

"Yes, Your Honour."

The next day, the defence called its first witness, Professor John Weiss, of the Wilfrid Laurier University's Business and Economics Department.

"Professor Weiss, you teach taxation at the university, correct?" asked Mark MacPharland.

"That is correct."

"And you are also an expert in the subject of taxation throughout history, and in particular the various types of resistance movements throughout, correct?"

"That is correct."

"Please give the court some examples of the types of resistance."

"Well, resistance to taxation has gone on as long as governments have imposed taxes. We can trace resistance movements back at least until the first century, current era. I suppose the best-known example is the so-called Boston Tea Party, when Britain imposed a tax on the American colonists and they reacted by raiding ships and throwing cartons of tea overboard. But there have many, many others throughout history.

"For instance, the story of Lady Godiva riding naked on a horse throughout the town is common knowledge, but do we know why? Well, that was a form of tax resistance. She was married to the Earl of Coventry, in the tenth century England. She had apparently pleaded with her husband to reduce taxes on the people of Coventry. Her husband, doubting the strength of her commitment, told her he would do so if she were to ride naked on a horse through the town. She called his bluff, and he reduced the taxes.

"Yet another creative example was resistance to the Window Tax. This was a form of wealth tax based on the number of windows in a house. The idea being that the wealthier an individual was, the bigger the house and therefore the more windows it would have. This tax was applied during the eighteenth and nineteenth centuries in the British Isles and some European countries. If you travel through those countries today you can see the windows that were removed and replaced by brick or stone in order to reduce the amount of tax the owner had to pay. The government didn't tell people they couldn't do that and so the revenue collected due to this resistance wasn't as much as it could have been."

Interrupting, Mr. Harris said, "Your Honour, I think we get the picture—"

"Your Honour, I think we should let the professor finish, he is coming to the point momentarily with some more modern examples," replied Mark MacPharland.

"All right, Mr. MacPharland, while I agree with Mr. Harris, I'll let the witness continue for the moment, but we need something more on point with respect to your client. You may continue, Professor Weiss."

"Thank you, Your Honour. Turning to more recent history, in 1906 the Doukhobors in western Canada refused to pay school taxes on the basis that they did not educate their children, 'lest they learn something evil'. And we can look to the women's suffrage movement in Britain and the United States as modern examples. They used tax resistance as a tool towards getting the vote on the basis of no taxation without representation—a throwback to the American Revolution. And then there is the Society of Friends—the Quakers as well as the Amish or Mennonites and their lower-key to resistance to paying taxes to support the military or to pay for wars. But I think you get the picture."

"Thank you, Professor Weiss. Does the Crown have any questions for this witness?"

Samantha Yang replied, "Yes, your Honour. Professor, the examples you used were essentially movements by many people to protest a certain type of taxation. For example, the bricking up of windows wasn't illegal, it was simply a way of reducing the impact of the widow tax by reducing the number of windows. Correct?"

"Yes, that is correct."

"Now, I wasn't aware of the story behind Lady Godiva's ride, but again that seems that one person undertook to do something and the government—the earl in this case—agreed to reduced the tax on the people of Coventry if that person, Lady Godiva, did as she said she would. Again, no illegal activity was involved."

"Correct," responded the professor.

"Now, in Canada we do have a legal system of taxation. A system that was introduced as a temporary measure to help pay for the First World War and then made permanent in 1949. In fact, the constitutional authority for the federal income tax can be found in section 91 paragraph 3 of the Constitution Act, 1867, formerly the British North America Act. That section assigns to the federal Parliament power over 'The raising of Money by any Mode or System of Taxation'.

"Similarly, the authority for the various provincial income taxes is found in section 92 paragraph 2 of the Constitution Act, which assigns to the legislature of each province the power of directly taxing residents for the purpose of raising revenue for provincial purposes.

"Correct, professor."

"Yes, that is correct."

"So, in Mr. Gerber's case, there is no defined movement he is supporting with respect to his failure to declare his income or remit tax, is there?"

"Not so far as I'm aware," answered the deflated professor.

"Thank you, professor. Those are all the questions I have, Your Honour."

"Professor Weiss, thank you. You are excused. Mr. Brock, do you have another witness?"

"Yes, Your Honour. Mr. Gerber would like to take the stand to explain his own rationale for not reporting his income or paying his income taxes."

"All right, but we'll take a break for lunch and reconvene at one-thirty."

CHAPTER 36

"Mr. Gerber, please tell the court, in your own words, why you to decided not to pay the taxes, as required by law."

"Thank you, Mr. Brock. To begin, I am a proud Canadian but, in many respects, I disagree with how the governments—both federal and provincial—spend *our* money. Yes, I said our money. We pay taxes, but we also elect the government and the government has, in my opinion—and in the opinions of many others, to spend the money we provide through the form of taxation in a responsible manner.

"While we heard from Professor Weiss that some people, such as the Quakers and Mennonites object to taxation for military spending, I am of the opposite view. I find that Canada's military procurement program is broken and costs taxpayers far more than it should to get the equipment our men and women in the military need. We look for so-called industrial offsets when looking for new equipment. We have a tremendously long bidding process and when we can't get what we want for the price we want, we reconfigure the requirements to meet the price. Rather, we should be looking to get the best equipment we can and not worry about industrial offsets.

"As an example, recently a potato chip factory was opened in Alberta as an 'offset' for equipment proposed to be bought from an

American supplier for a ship-building program. Now, does anyone really think that a potato chip factory is really bringing high tech jobs to offset a purchase of technology from a foreign supplier?

"And the government does spend wastefully. The government, whichever party is in power, tends to provide funding on a partisan political basis. Consider building a cheese factory in Quebec or providing $2.5 billion to a grocery chain—owned by a billionaire no less—to provide better refrigeration for certain foods. Why give money to the rich when we have many who live below the poverty line? In fact, you could say the government uses taxpayers' as an ATM tor partisan political purposes, rather than trying to get the best value they can for Canadians.

"And it is no different provincially. Those governments should be concentrating on health care, education, and spending on maintaining our roads and power systems instead of giving money to corporations to supposedly keep jobs in the province. At some point, companies make the best decisions for themselves and if they want to close a plant, they close a plant. We give them money, so they postpone the decision for a few years.

"I could go on, but I hope the court understands my frustration and why I choose not to pay taxes on my income."

"Thank you, Mr. Gerber. Mr. Harris, do you have any questions for the witness?"

"Yes, Your Honour. Mr. Gerber, you have a master's degree in economics and taught income tax at a university for five years, is that correct?"

"Yes."

"But you say you aren't remitting taxes as required by law, and by the Canadian Constitution because you disagree with how the government is spending 'your' money. But surely there must be better ways to make your concerns known, especially given your background—"

"Your Honour, is there a question in there or is the Crown already into his closing argument?"

"Mr. Harris?"

"Sorry Your Honour, I was getting to the question."

"Move a little more quickly, sir."

"Yes, Your Honour. Mr. Gerber, did you ever consider contacting your MP about your concerns?"

"Yes. And I did. But back benchers are little more that spear carriers—"

"Spear carriers?" interrupted Mr. Harris.

"Yes, you know, foot soldiers. They get elected, the government gets a majority or a minority and then the big shots—the PM and his ministers make the decisions. Or today, it's the PM's office as likely as not and the ministers carry out its orders. No, backbenchers have no control or input into government policy."

"So why not write a letter to the editor of your local paper, or even a national paper?"

"Do you think the government really pays attention to editorials? No one reads newspapers anymore. It's all podcasts or online news. And young people, they don't pay any attention, they're to busy with tweeting or looking at online dribble. No, the only way to get the government's attention is through direct action. Withhold taxes!"

"So why not start a movement?"

"There is really no organization to do that."

"Oh, I see. So instead of starting one you just decide not to pay your fair share, you decide to hide your income in art work, or in investments in the United States, even going so far as to get an American passport—which by the way is illegal—and smuggling—yes that is the word—smuggling your ill-gotten gains offshore. That sounds to me like a tax evader, not some sort of patriot who is not paying taxes legally payable in order to make some sort of point… and more than that, you also hide money offshore. Using Bitcoin to get money out of the country and open a foreign bank and investment accounts—"

"Your Honour, is there a question in there?" interrupted counsel for the defence.

"Sorry, Your Honour, I have no further questions for this witness!" answered Mr. Harris before the judge could speak.

"The witness may step down. Mr. Brock, do you have any more witnesses?"

"No, Your Honour."

"Fine, closing arguments tomorrow morning, 9:00 a.m. sharp."

CHAPTER 37

"Mr. Brock, are you ready to proceed?"

"Yes, Your Honour. While my client, Mr. Gerber, admits that he did not pay his taxes, and admittedly went to great lengths to avoid paying taxes, he did so because he did not believe that the government of Canada was using those monies collected, in the best interests of Canadians. The money was being wastefully spent. The government—any government—held bidding competition after competition for military hardware while the men and women who volunteered to serve their country were left wanting. And where supposed industrial offsets were obtained, they weren't necessarily of the type that increased Canada's technological capability. Witness the potato chip factory in Alberta in return for buying American high-tech capability for the navy.

"Did he do it the 'right way'? Perhaps not. He did not galvanize broad support for his protest, but advertising a protest, such as his, would have been hard, if not impossible to do, as the CRA would have learned of it quickly. But he did do what he thought was appropriate for a personal protest.

"So, I ask the Court to take that into consideration and to waive the interest and penalties that have been assessed to ensure that, while he may have to pay the taxes owing, that the continuing increasing burden of the interest accruing be limited, if not eliminated.

"As well, we ask the court to consider his motives in not paying tax or filing tax returns and to find him not guilty on the charges of tax evasion and money laundering. Yes, he did move money to the United States illegally, but he did it so as part of his tax protest. We request that you give him a conditional discharge, or if you find him guilty, then give him no jail time or fine.

"Thank you, Your Honour. The defence rests."

"Mr. Harris?"

"Thank you, Your Honour. Mr. Brock tried to persuade the court that Mr. Gerber's act of tax evasion—not avoidance—was done in the manner of protest for the way the governments, both federal and provincial, spends their revenue from the proper collection of income taxes. And I emphasize again, this is a case of tax evasion and not avoidance. A simple, and permissible, example of legal tax avoidance is contributing money to a Registered Retirement Savings Plan. The money contributed results in a tax deduction, and when the funds are withdrawn, they are taxed then, and at a presumably lower rate. Another example is the use of the Tax-Free Savings Account. There is no tax deduction when the money is contributed, but the income earned is not subject to taxation.

"Similarly, the us of trusts or corporations, where there is a legitimate purpose for those structures is also an acceptable way for people to minimize taxation.

"And where the CRA finds that the means the taxpayer used to avoid tax, there is the General Anti-Avoidance Rule in the Income Tax Act, that can be applied.

"But, in Mr. Gerber's case, he didn't avoid paying tax through allowable methods, rather he failed to file tax returns, took steps to hide his income, and moved funds offshore. In short, tax evasion is deliberately ignoring the laws of the country. And, in addition, he did it using a false American passport.

"Mr. Gerber deliberately failed to report income from his business. In fact, he structured those businesses so that all he received was the net revenue and the client companies actually paid the expenses. He set up a US bank account and investment account to move money offshore using the fraudulent US passport. He bought antiques and helped his girlfriend pay her mortgage.

"No, Your Honour, this is not an example of a tax protest, but the wilful evasion of income taxes. The hiding of funds, and the using of a false identity, clearly show that this was a criminal activity and should be punished accordingly.

"The Crown asks that not only the client be subject to the taxes, penalties, and interest assessed but the also be sentenced to jail for a term prescribed by law for tax evasion and money laundering. In addition, he should be subject to the maximum fines allowed by law for those crimes.

"We also request that the Court impose a separate sentence with respect to the charges of money laundering and using a false identity and passport.

"Your Honour, the Crown rests."

"Thank you, gentlemen. We will reconvene a week from next Monday at 10 a.m. I'll render my verdict at that time."

CHAPTER 38

At the appointed time the court reconvened, Madam Justice Barbara Laughlin presiding.

"Mr. Gerber, while I may personally sympathise with some of your concerns about government waste, the way you went about your protest was both inappropriate and illegal. You have an obligation to pay taxes on your income as well as sales taxes, as prescribed by the laws of the country.

"We have mechanisms to protest legitimately. You can do that at the ballot box; by raising issues with your member of parliament; by writing letters to the editor; by setting up a webpage where people of similar opinions can share their frustrations and concerns and then taking those concerns to the government. You are also charged with money laundering and using a false identity and a fraudulently obtained American passport.

"You have the ability to legally divert some, if not all of your taxes owing, to worthy causes through charitable giving. You could have donated to any number of charities that do good works and to some that help those injured serving our country.

"But you, sir, wilfully evaded paying the taxes you owed and took steps, and some that required significant planning, to hide your income. And now it's time to pay the piper.

"I find that the penalties and interest assessed by the Canada Revenue Agency stand. I also find you guilty on the separate charges of tax evasion and money laundering. The way you went about hiding the funds you received shows willful intent and given your education and background in economics and tax, you clearly knew what you were doing was illegal.

"You went to great lengths to evade the taxes owing, resulting in both investigations not only by our authorities, but by the American Internal Revenue Service as well.

"For the failure to file returns for income tax as well as failure to file harmonized sales tax returns, I am sentencing you to one year in jail. I also fine you $50,000 on that charge.

"In addition, with respect to the charge of tax evasion, you are sentenced to one year in jail. On the charge of money laundering, I sentence you to one year in jail, to be served concurrently with the sentence for tax evasion, along with an additional fine of $50,000.

"You, sir, should be ashamed of yourself—"

"Madam Justice," interrupted Samuel Brock, "If I may, I request that the commencement of my client's sentence be deferred for at least 30 days so he can put his affairs in order."

Before Justice Laughlin could respond, Mr. Harris, the Crown attorney was on his feet. "Madam Justice. The crown will agree to the 30-day grace period, provided, *provided* that Mr. Gerber is prepared take a trip to New York City and arrange for the funds invested there to be transferred back to Canada, and preferably directly to his tax account with the CRA."

"Mr. Harris, Mr. Gerber has surrendered his passports. How do you propose he go to the United States? Do you simply propose to give him back his identification and trust him?"

"Of course not, Your Honour. We would send an escort with him who would ensure he did as he was required and return home. This could be a collections officer from the CRA or an RCMP officer."

"Madam Justice, I object to the Crown's suggestion," stated Mr. Brock emphatically.

"Why?"

"If my client returns to the United States, the IRS is well aware of his accounts and they, or another alphabet agency, may arrest my client for using a false passport. And the penalties there could be severe."

"Well sir, as I see it, your client went to great lengths to hide his earnings and not pay the requisite taxes on those earnings. And I agree with the Crown that those funds should be repatriated.

"I direct that you and Mr. Harris work together to see if the funds can be repatriated without the need for Mr. Gerber go to New York in person. But, if not, or if the procedure would be too time consuming, then Mr. Gerber will have to go in person, with an escort as recommended by the Crown, to close those accounts.

"As to the 30-day period for Mr. Gerber to get his affairs in order, I am in agreement and it is so ordered. I also will put in a stipulation that if his personal attendance at the New York bank is required, he may be released from jail in the custody of a law enforcement officer for no more than five days so that he may close out his US accounts.

"If there is no further business…"

"No, Your Honour."

"No, Your Honour."

"Then I will refer this case to Correctional Services to determine the appropriate detention centre and confirm the 30-day grace period." Turning to face Gerber, she went on, "Mr. Gerber, you have been given 30 days to get your affairs in order. Don't abuse it! Court is adjourned."

CHAPTER 39

Two days later, Samuel Brock and Trevor Harris met in a café, along with Hans Kaufman, the Director of the Collections unit in Kitchener, to discuss obtaining the US funds. Mr. Brock was concerned about Gerber's exposure to arrest in New York for using a false passport. And while there was some, if little, sympathy from Harris and Kaufman their main concern was getting the funds as soon as possible. There was at least $593,500 US in the bank in both investment and savings accounts. That translated to about $742,000 Canadian. That would settle about a third of the outstanding taxes, interest, and penalties. The sale of the seized diamonds might generate upwards of another $500,000. It would then be a matter of finding the balance. Kaufman suggested that seizing the works of art and collectables might satisfy a lot of the balance, depending what the actual sales brought in.

"So how do we go about getting the US funds?" asked Brock.

"Well, we can issue a Requirement to Pay," replied Kaufman. But it is a foreign bank located in a foreign country. While we have good relations with the IRS and share information with them about American citizens with Canadian accounts and they reciprocate, I'm not sure that will carry a lot of weight with a bank located in the

US I'll get hold of our deputy minister and ask him to contact his counterpart in Washington.

"And, with respect to the diamonds, we will issue a Requirement to the Crown Attorney's office just to cover off any possibility that Mr. Gerber has an objection."

Brock cleared his throat "Umm, pardon me. I don't like to sound petty, but Mr. Gerber owes me and Mr. MacPharland in the neighbourhood of $250,000 for his defence. And we need to get paid as well."

"Sam, I appreciate the position you're in," stated Harris, "but the Crown's claims take precedence. I suggest you file a claim with the court and with Collections to be compensated. I know that that doesn't help you immediately. Perhaps you can talk to Gerber's partner, Jacqueline Mendes and see if she can pay you. After all, some of his ill-gotten gains went to help pay her mortgage."

"Speaking of Ms. Mendes," interrupted Brock, "why didn't she ever show up in court? I called her a couple of times and asked her to come as I thought her presence might at least elicit some sympathy from the bench."

Harris replied, "I wondered that myself. I suspect that she was very upset at having been lied to by a man she trusted, loved, and lived with. Especially the finding of the safe that had been installed in her house unbeknownst to her. I really do think she was taken advantage of by Gerber, and I hope she gets some counselling. But he did help her pay for a house and she benefited from that, so you would be in your rights to put a lien against the house to get paid."

CHAPTER 40

Three weeks later, the three reconvened in the same café across from Kitchener City Hall.

"Well, Hans, what does Collections have to say?" asked Samuel Brock.

"Well, the DM talked to his counterpart at the IRS. They have no objection with us serving a Requirement on the bank in New York City. He recommends we send a collections officer and he will arrange for that person to be met at the airport by an IRS equivalent to accompany him or her to the bank and confirm the request has been approved by the IRS. It really doesn't have to be, but the way things are politically down there, he felt it would be prudent. And Mr. Brock, the DM also said that the $75,000 that was seized from Gerber's safe can be paid to you as a partial settlement of Gerber's debt to you and Mr. MacPharland."

"That's good news! Thank you. At least that will cover many of the direct expenses we've incurred on Gerber's behalf. And I did take your advice and I've filed a lien against Mendes' new house so at least she can't sell it without me getting paid! I'll amend the lien, and I'll talk to her about paying me. I'll also contact Collections and file a lien with them if more money is found than is required to fund the government's debt."

"Consider it done," replied Kaufman, handing Brock a sheet of paper and asking him to sign and date it.

The following week, CRA Collections Officer Suzanne Greer arrived at New York's Newark airport on a flight from Toronto's Island Airport accompanied by a constable from the RCMP's commercial crimes branch. They were met by Tony Gelatin of the IRS's Criminal Special Investigations unit. Together they went to the Third Manhattan Bank of New York where Ms. Greer presented the Requirement to Pay and the IRS agent confirmed it was correct and in order. He also gave the manger the key to the safe deposit box obtained from Gerber. The manger said that it would take some time to liquidate the investments held by Gerber's nom de plume, Warren White. So, after a pleasant lunch at a nearby Five Napkin Burger, they returned and the manager handed Ms. Greer a bank draft, in the amount of USD$650,830.22, payable to the Receiver General for Canada, along with the diamonds contained in a black leather pouch.

"Thank you," replied Ms. Greer, putting the cheque and diamonds in her purse. This was more than the anticipated amount. But, she realized, that was the value when the audit was conducted so the investment growth since had not been taken into account. This would go a long way to settling the outstanding tax liability and additional penalties when it was translated into Canadian dollars.

Epilogue

Harold Gerber started to serve his consecutive sentences at a minimum-security institution in Gravenhurst, Ontario. Six months after Gerber started his sentence, the Attorney General for Canada received an extradition request from her counterpart in the United States requesting Gerber be extradited to the United States after his prison sentence to be charged with using a false United States passport. If convicted, he could be subject to a US federal prison sentence of up to ten years. He never heard from Jaqueline Mendes again.

Jacqueline Mendes sold her new house in New Hamburg and paid Samuel Brock the outstanding balance of his legal fees, although those were not as high as first anticipated due to the higher amount of funds received from the US to help settle Gerber's outstanding liabilities. She moved to another city without leaving a forwarding address.

Tom Thomas was assigned to the Major Tax Fraud unit within Special Investigations. While still located in the Kitchener office, he would be involved in national cases with broad tax fraud and evasion implications.

Al Edwards was promoted to a more senior audit position and the director suggested that, after a couple of more years working on more complex files, he should consider applying to Special Investigations.

THE END

About the author

This is Ted Ballantyne's first novel. It draws from his background of thirty-two years in the financial services industry where he had interactions with the Canada Revenue Agency on matters of interpretation and with the Department of Finance on tax policy issues affecting personal financial and retirement planning.

He has an Honours Bachelor's degree in Business Administration from Wilfrid Laurier University and a Masters of Law (Taxation) from York University's Osgoode Hall Law School. He is also a Chartered Professional Accountant (retired).

Ted lives in Kitchener, Ontario with his wife and life partner, Jane. They have three adult children and one grandson.

CPSIA information can be obtained
at www.ICGtesting.com
Printed in the USA
LVHW041031220721
693398LV00003B/323

9 781525 582035